The Star-Fighters
of Murphy Street

ESCAPE
from the
Drooling Octopod!

Escape from the Drooling Octopod!
Copyright © 2008 by Robert West
Illustrations © 2008 by C.B. Canga

Requests for information should be addressed to:
Zonderkidz, *Grand Rapids, Michigan* 49530

Library of Congress Cataloging-in-Publication Data: Applied for
ISBN 978-0-310-71427-9

Published in association with the literary agency of WordServe Literary Group, Ltd.,
10152 S. Knoll Circle, Highlands Ranch, CO 80130.

Zonderkidz is a trademark of Zondervan.

Editor: *Barbara Scott*
Art direction & cover design: *Merit Alderink*
Interior design: *Carlos Eluterio Estrada*

Printed in the United States of America

08 09 10 11 12 • 5 4 3 2 1

Escape from the Drooling Octopod!

Robert West

ZONDERVAN.com/
AUTHORTRACKER
follow your favorite authors

For my wife, Helen, whose gentle patience and love were always more support than I could deserve, and for my three sons, Chris, Robbie, and David—each so unique in personality but who share qualities of idealism, intellectual honesty, and an appreciation of life that continually make me proud beyond reason.

-RW

Table of Contents

1

Flight of the Pink Carpet

Beamer didn't have a clue where he was. He just woke up and ... *boing!*—he was circling in the air around a castle. He'd have preferred an F–18 or a stealth fighter. What did he get? A flying carpet. Talk about obsolete! He could forget Mach one. "Skateboard one" was probably pushing it. What was worse, the carpet had a temper. *How do you hang on to these things?* "Whoa!" he yelped as he was suddenly flipped into the air. He managed to grab hold of the carpet's fringe just as it dived through a large window in the castle. "Whaaaaooooooooooo," he exclaimed as his stomach turned inside out.

Incidentally, the castle was pink ... yeah, pink, as in bubble gum, peppermint sticks, and Barbie toys. Come to think of it, so was the carpet—pink, that is. He hated pink. That was the color his big sister, Erin, wore all the time. Frankly, if he wasn't dipping through the hallways of the castle and holding on for dear life, he'd never have taken a flying pink carpet seriously.

The next thing Beamer knew, he was on the floor looking up at a pink crystal chandelier about the size of his house. *Whoa! If that thing falls on me, I'll be a sparkly porcupine—not to mention dead.* It seemed like a good idea to get out from under it, but, for some reason, he couldn't move. He felt like he was wearing a straitjacket. He tried to wiggle free—no such luck. Then he looked down. That rascally carpet had wrapped around him like a cocoon. *Great! Now he was a bug in a rug!* "A little breathing room, please!" he called out to the carpet.

That was when Beamer noticed that he was rolled up at the foot of a huge pink staircase. It was shaped sort of like an hourglass, narrower in the middle than at the top or bottom. For all he knew, this could have been the very staircase where Cinderella lost her glass slipper. Why anyone would wear a glass slipper was beyond him. One step is all it would take for his sister to crunch it into smithereens. *Then she could forget being found by the prince who was posing as a would-be shoe salesman. Of course, if the only way this prince guy could recognize her was by her shoe size, he probably needed glasses as thick as binoculars. Either that or the fairy's spell on Cinderella included some major plastic surgery.*

Suddenly Beamer heard loud crunching and splintering. He jerked his head up to see an elephant swinging on the chandelier. Yep, you guessed it—a pink elephant! The big pachyderm was filling the air with pink glass like a hailstorm.

Then Beamer heard something groaning and then wailing in a high pitch. *The chandelier is about to fall!* Beamer twisted and turned, trying to get the carpet rolling. But instead of rolling across the room, he started rolling up the stairs! *Hey, what happened to gravity? You can't roll up stairs!* But then, what else could he expect from a flying carpet? "Ow! Ow! Hey! Whoa!" he yelped as he bumped along, lickety-split, up the stairs. The staircase must have been much taller than he thought. He just kept on bumping and rolling without coming to the top of the stairs. Of course, he wasn't seeing things all that well. Spinning around in that rug was making him pretty dizzy. Everything was swirling around like a pink tornado.

Beamer finally thudded to a stop. As the whirl of pink in his head slowed down, he noticed that he was no longer on the stairs. He also began having second thoughts about what he was wrapped up in. It wasn't a rug or a carpet or a straitjacket anymore. He was in a cocoon—a pink cocoon! What was worse, he was stuck in the middle of a huge pink spiderweb! He twisted and kicked, trying to break out of the cocoon. The web shook beneath him. Pretty soon it was shaking even more. He strained to tilt his head back. Then he saw it—a pink nightmare whose eight legs were churning in perfect order across the web. Soon he was going to be one big Slurpee for that hairy spider behemoth.

Soon it would be all over—no obituary, no tombstone, no nothing. Since none of this could possibly be real, Beamer MacIntyre wasn't even going to be history—he was just one more fantasy character crumpled and tossed into the trash can. He flailed about one last time, trying to escape—

Beamer thumped on a hard surface. "Ow!" he yelped in pain. Anxiously, he fought the confinement of the cocoon. Finally, he threw it off. But it wasn't a cocoon anymore. It was a blanket—his sister's pink quilt! *Yech! No wonder everything was pink.* His blanket must have been in the wash and his mom snuck his sister's on his bed under the bedspread. He looked up and saw the ceiling with the ice-cream-cone water stain. He was back in his bedroom, on the floor next to his bed. *It was all a dream—a silly old dream.* He sighed. *Talk about twisted fairy tales!*

"Beamer, you'll be late for school!" his mom called from

the kitchen downstairs. "Stove, plate fo'ah low. Toastah own!" he heard her say. The only way to get the kitchen appliances to work in this house was to talk to them. But you had to talk to them nicely and in a Southern accent. Californian wouldn't cut it. That's where Beamer had come from—California. Living on Murphy Street in Middle America was turning out to be a whole new ball game.

"Mo-o-o-o-ommm!" a shrill voice shouted at the same time. "Where are my pink Nikes?" It was Beamer's big sister, Erin, otherwise known as Zero, Zero, Zero (0,0,0). Those are the coordinates for the center of the universe, which is what she thought she was. It was totally disgusting. As far as she was concerned, everyone and everything else in the universe revolved around her.

Also, at the same time, Beamer heard alternating thumping and slapping sounds on the staircase. That was the sound of a strange quadruped named Michael, his nine-year-old brother, who always came up the steps on all fours.

The last set of sounds came from his dad in the shower: "Too hot, too hot!" he said to the plumbing. "*Caolder, caolder, caolder . . . ahhhh, jaust raight.*"

This was why Beamer didn't have many sleepovers at his house.

*   *   *   *   *

During history class, it finally occurred to Beamer where at least part of his dream had come from. It should have been obvious. *It was the web!—his web!* Nearly two stories tall and as wide as the house, the famous MacIntyre Web was the nightmare in the attic—the greatest entomological mystery this side of Cleveland.

Up until Christmas, the scientists experimenting on the web

in their attic weren't even sure that it was a real web. Some thought it was man-made, somebody's joke or a hobby project or a mad scientist's experiment. But back on Christmas Eve, Molgotha, the web maker, had returned. She'd spun a cocoon around every piece of scientific equipment surrounding the web. Then she sucked the electronic life out of them, leaving them totally useless, as dead as the flies in the little web under the corner gutter.

So now, scientists from all over the country were in the MacIntyre attic, hovering around the web, hooking up this and that sensor. More than ever, the attic looked like the bridge of Darth Vader's Star Destroyer. Cameras now monitored the web 24–7, and multiple alarm systems registered every movement. The only reason the MacIntyres were still willing and able to live in the house was because the scientists calculated that all of the security systems gave the spider only "one chance in a hundred" of getting down where they lived. Of course, that "one chance in a hundred" was covered by family prayers every night. How many spiders do you know of that get into people's prayers?

That was three months ago. Spring vacation was only a half circle of the moon away, and still nobody knew who or why or what Molgotha was all about. Part of Beamer hoped they never would. It was kind of cool having a big mystery in your attic, except for the fact that it gave you the heebie-jeebies every time you got near it. You could never lose the feeling that Molgotha was up there somewhere, hiding in the shadows, smackin' her chops for your yummy red corpuscles.

His history teacher interrupted Beamer's little day-dream with a question. Unfortunately, he didn't hear the question—something you could never admit doing in Mrs. Hotchkiss's class. She wasn't called "the drill sergeant" for nothing. Beamer hemmed and hawed, tugging at his polo-shirt collar. He'd read the assignment, for Pete's sake. "Uh, could you repeat the question, please?" he asked sheepishly. "I ... uh just missed the last couple of words."

"Murphy Street," his teacher said simply.

"Huh?" Beamer asked, remembering nothing about Murphy Street in his history lesson.

"Isn't that where you live—Murphy Street?" she asked, growing impatient.

"Uh ... yes, ma'am, that's where I live all right," he said with a fake smile.

"Good," Mrs. Hotchkiss said. "Come by my desk on your way out. I have a little favor to ask of you."

Beamer groaned. A favor for Mrs. Hotchkiss could be anything from banging chalk out of the erasers until you were coated white to making a full-scale papier-mâché statue of Genghis Khan.

2

Missing: Beauty and the Beast

As it turned out, Mrs. Hotchkiss only wanted him to drop off some study guides for a homeschool student who lived on Murphy Street. Beamer's friend and tomboy neighbor, Scilla, and his brother, Michael, were with him on the way home, as usual. Their friend Ghoulie had already split off for his place. When they got to the address his teacher had given him, all Beamer could see was a huge hedge. They found a walk-in gate. Beamer started to push the call button but bumped the gate. It swung open, so they went on in.

One thing became clear right off: neither his mom nor his dad could ever be allowed to see this yard. It would be "all she wrote" for weekend playtime. If they tried to match this yard, he'd be drafted into slave-labor yard duty up to the age of thirty.

You see, this yard was perfect. Every blade of grass was in place and as green as green could get. Plants and bushes (flowering and otherwise) were perfectly trimmed, and the brick walkway was lined with flowers spaced evenly apart like marching soldiers.

The walkway wound to the right and then to the left and then finally through a row of Italian cypress trees—you know, the trees that look like narrow green flames rising up from the ground. That's when they saw it. Scilla gulped with her mouth open. Michael covered his eyes and looked between his fingers. It was a house guaranteed to make you diabetic at first sight.

Actually, it looked like a giant birthday cake—a very *pink* birthday cake. Beamer groaned as memories of his pink dream rolled around in his head like a loose marble. There were no sharp corners on the house. Everything was rounded off—walls, the tops of windows, and doors—and decorated with fanciful little flower and plant designs. If he hadn't been sure the walls were made of stone, he'd have taken a lick or two. But then pink icing wasn't exactly his favorite.

They walked up a short flight of steps onto a small but elegant porch with columns on either side. Beamer pushed the doorbell. They heard a musical ring inside, but no one came to the door. After a few moments, Beamer pushed it again. Still no one answered. Beamer looked around for someplace to leave the papers, but Michael jumped up next to him and punched the doorbell several times like it was a pinball machine.

"Hey!" Beamer yelped at him. "If they hadn't heard it already, they're probably asleep and won't appreciate being woke up."

Just then someone opened the door. Beamer had his back to the door at that moment and turned only in time to see a fluffy sleeve and the corner of a frilly dress disappear. Beamer could feel a gust from the rush of movement inside. A young girl had opened the door—he was sure of it—but in a switcheroo move as quick as a magician with a rabbit in his hat, she was gone.

The person who now appeared in the pink doorway had dark blonde hair rolled up in a bun—definitely not a little girl. She wore wire-rimmed glasses balanced on a pointed nose.

"Children, you should have rung me *befoah* coming into the *yahd*," the woman said, a little flushed from alarm. Her words sounded funny. She definitely wasn't from Middleton. "I'm *sahry*. I don't mean to be rude," she said nervously as she shoved her glasses back up on her nose. "What do you want?"

"Ah … well, my teacher, Mrs. Hotchkiss, asked me to drop off these papers for you." Beamer noticed the picture of a little girl on the wall in the background. *Was that the little girl she had yanked away from the door so quickly? She didn't look more than six or seven.*

"Oh, of *coahse*," the woman said as she took the papers and flipped through them. "Thank you very much for dropping them by. *Heah*, let me give you something for *yoah* trouble," she added as she moved quickly back inside the house.

"That's all right," Beamer called to her. "I live just down the street. It was on my way home." Beamer had run through his mental database of movie characters and concluded that the woman talked like Mary Poppins. She was a magical nanny from England. He didn't see an umbrella, though, and guessed that this English nanny probably couldn't fly like Mary Poppins could.

"Well, that's *vahry* kind of you," she said as she returned to the doorway. "Please pull the gate closed when you leave," she said as she started to close the door. "It is supposed to stay locked. Bye now." Her parting smile was about as sickly sweet as the house.

Beamer and Scilla gave each other questioning looks. Beamer could tell that Scilla was thinking about the same person he was thinking about—someone else who had shooed them away from a door. The memory of the overprotective Mrs. Drummond and her sisters was still very clear in their minds. Those ladies had kept Solomon Parker locked up and hidden from the world so that they could use his great wealth. Was something like that going on with the girl in this house?

"Hey, what's the holdup?" Michael asked impatiently.

Beamer shook his head and rolled his eyes. "Aw, come on, we're just being paranoid."

* * * * *

Now that the days were stretching longer, Beamer had a little extra time to spend in the tree ship after school. The tree was sprouting leaf buds like goose bumps, and Beamer was beginning to hear the chirping and chittering of birds and squirrels. He'd listened for the crickets, but Ghoulie told him that a lot of insects, including the crickets, wouldn't come out for another month or two.

As he climbed up the tree in his backyard, he wondered what the old broken-down trolley station looked like now. Last winter the snow cover had given it a kind of magical look. Of course, whatever it looked like now, it wasn't going to stay that way. Solomon Parker was already working on plans to revive his trolley business for tourists. Why anybody would want to tour Middleton was beyond Beamer. *It's not like it is Disneyland.*

Solomon Parker's trolley company had gone out of business fifty years ago when buses replaced trolleys on city streets. Although he was a genius who built amazing inventions, like spidery robots and hovering trains, nobody believed they could really work. He finally got so discouraged that he lost all faith in himself and in God. He became a hermit in his own house, exiled to the ballroom on the second floor of his mansion. He was left there amid gathering dust and cobwebs by his house-keeper, who took over his home affairs while he wallowed in depression. Meanwhile, his investment in a railroad grew over the years until he was very wealthy, but his housekeeper hid the truth from him while she and her two identical sisters lived in luxury.

With the help of Beamer, Scilla, and Ghoulie, Solomon got his life back on course and booted the evil triplets out of his home. Now, Solomon had his own railroad and a city that was willing to listen to his ideas.

Beamer didn't know what he wanted to be yet—maybe a SWAT team member or an operative (isn't that what they call a spy now?) for the CIA. *Astronaut* had a good ring to it if you could actually do some real exploring. Scientists were doing most of the exploring these days—in test tubes, accelerators, telescopes, and remote-controlled probes. Everything was viewed on monitors instead of up close and personal. You'd have thought the whole universe was virtual instead of real.

Of course that wasn't a problem for the Star-Fighters. Already in their tree ship they'd visited exploding planets, space platforms operated by robots, and ice moons with ice castles. They'd rubbed shoulders (or ... whatever) with intelligent insects and cat-like humanoids.

From his spot in the tree in his yard, Beamer could see into the attic windows. He couldn't see the web inside. In fact, he hadn't even been allowed in the attic since the attack on the machines. *What kind of a spider sucks the power out of a machine?* The scientists had been able to prove that the spider was no longer in the house. But how did she get in, and where did she go when she left? Of course, there were also a lot of other questions that began with the word *why*.

Most spiders, of course, could get into a house through any little crack or cranny, but that wouldn't hold for Molgotha. She was definitely one big mama! Judging from the size of the web fibers, the bug scientist guys had figured that the spider had a body anywhere from three feet to five feet in diameter. It seemed to Beamer that somebody would have probably noticed a giant spider strolling down the street. I mean, you add eight splayed-out legs to that body, and you have something right out of a Saturday-night monster flick clomping down the block.

So, if she didn't escape down the street, how did she escape? Beamer wondered. The wind suddenly picked up, making him rock and roll with the branches. A chill suddenly ran through Beamer's limbs like an electrical shock. What if she made her escapes through a tree—as in this tree? Beamer's eyes suddenly grew as big as fried eggs. He shot into the tree ship and slammed the door behind him. He then whammed all the windows shut, leaving one cracked open only enough for one scared eye to peak through.

The wind stopped blowing, but he still heard the sound of creaking branches from somewhere. The sound got louder as more branches scratched each other. *Something was coming!* Suddenly he heard scuffling and a loud *thump* that shook the tree ship. A long thin something, about the shape of a giant spider leg, slapped the window point-blank in front of his eye. He slammed the window closed and lunged backward across the room. "Aiiiiii!" he screeched before he smacked into a plywood control panel. At the same time he heard a *bang*, followed by a blinding blast of light.

3

Monsters of the Deep

"Beamer, are you having a fit or something?" asked the figure who stood with her hand on cocked hip, silhouetted in the bright doorway. It was Scilla. She had the cocking-her-hip thing down to a precision science these days.

"Hey, what do you think of my new fishing rod?" asked Ghoulie, who threw open a window and waved a fishing rod.

Fishing rod? Who brings a fishing rod into a tree? What'd he expect to catch, flying fish? Hey, it sort of looks like a giant spider leg. Anybody could have made the same mistake. Right? "Hey guys!" he said sheepishly. "I just figured something out!" Before he had time to say anything else, though, he heard a loud *whoosh!* He saw a spinning stream of colored light and suddenly felt like his stomach had turned into a washing machine.

Then it seemed like the whole ship was in a washing machine. They were spinning around in a pink-and-white whirlpool. A whole wave of pink liquid washed in the door

... air lock ... whatever ... and splashed Beamer into the bulk-head.

The captain leaned against the door and struggled to close it before more liquid could wash in. Then she brushed back her hair and touched a tiny disc to one side of her mouth. "Ives. Lieutenant Ives!" she yelled. "Turn on the pumps!"

Beamer spit out a mouthful of the pink water. "Yuck! It tastes like fruit punch—salty fruit punch," he said as he ran to the water dispenser. He gargled and spit out several cupfuls.

"Take it easy, MacIntyre," said Captain Bruzelski.

"But what if it's full of deadly bacteria or radioactive?" he asked, gargling another cup of water.

"Good question," she murmured.

Somewhere in the back of MacIntyre's mind, Beamer wondered what would happen if one of them died in one of their adventures. Would they die back in the real world too?

"Go ahead and gargle," the captain said. "Where's Lieutenant Ives?" she asked, looking around. "Ives!" she crowed again into her communicator. "What's happening with the pumps? Ives, where are you? Ives! Respond!"

Commander MacIntyre spit out one last gargle and charged after her onto the bridge. Static on the communicator was as loud as a heavy-metal band. Both he and Captain Bruzelski held their ears with a grimace. Then the static cleared: Lieutenant Ives's voice came in loud and clear.

"I'm out here, Captain," the lieutenant said. "The view is terrific!"

"There he is," said MacIntyre, pointing toward the main view screen.

The picture was something out of Captain Nemo's world. Bizarre rock formations were the setting for multiple schools of fish, which swam back and forth like competing drill teams. In the middle of them was the lieutenant in a hard diving suit, bobbing around like a beach ball with bubbles coming out of his helmet. He held some kind of speargun with a large fish squirming on the tip.

"What'd you catch?" the captain asked with a chuckle.

"Good question," the voice spoke through the ship's speakers. "With four eyes and four fins, it doesn't fit on any known-species chart."

The commander shook his head, momentarily remembering something about him having a fishing rod. Of course that was ridiculous; you can't fish with a fishing rod underwater.

At that moment the fish gave a frantic wiggle, broke loose from the speargun, and swam off. "Rats, I was looking forward to some lip-smacking fish and chips," the lieutenant said with a sigh.

"How about checking out that sunken ship behind you?" suggested the captain.

Right smack in the middle of those twisted and jumbled rocks was a shipwreck. MacIntyre didn't see a pirate flag, but it looked like it could have come right out of a pirate movie. The trouble was that the colors were all wrong. The shipwreck had torn light pink sails, a red hull with a big hole through it, and a thick coating of purple barnacles.

"MacIntyre, get those pumps working," the captain ordered as pink liquid washed across the floor.

The commander jumped to it. "Hey, since when did our spaceship become a submarine?"

"Multipurpose vehicle for a multifunctional universe," answered Bruzelski proudly.

Whew, that sounded impressive. Scilla definitely liked being in command. Of course, Beamer knew the feeling—on a tree-ship adventure, everything seemed to come into your head with hardly a moment's thought. The truth was that, just like him and Ghoulie, Scilla had only the slightest inkling of what her fantasy self was talking about. But then they had a few years yet to catch up, knowledge-wise, with their fantasy selves.

"Captain, we have to get out of here!" the lieutenant's voice shouted in alarm. "There's a whole school of something — something big — coming our way!"

"Yep, I've got them on sonar," yelled the commander.

"Get in here, Ives!" the captain ordered. "As in make like a fish! MacIntyre, open the starboard air lock." The ship began to lurch in the pink sea like a bobber on a fishing line.

"Look, Captain, on-screen!" MacIntyre shouted.

A huge shadow crawled across the seafloor in front of them. Then something gigantic grew in size at the top of the screen as it passed overhead. Before MacIntyre could take a second breath, the creature filled the screen.

Beamer thought of the opening scene in the first *Star Wars* movie—episode four, that is—when the huge Star Destroyer passed overhead. That long shot gave a sense of how huge the spaceship was. What was flying over them was no spaceship, though; this was a monstrous undersea creature.

It looked something like a giant manta ray and was about the size of a basketball court. With each dip of its enormous fins, it fanned the pink sea into a turbulent froth that tossed their ship about like a plastic toy in a bathtub.

"Captain, they're all around us," she heard the lieutenant gasp on the speakers.

Sure enough, to either side was a whole fleet of these creatures moving in a V formation. Suddenly they both heard and felt a bang on their hull. All at once they were tumbling around the walls and ceiling like jeans and T-shirts in a dryer.

The captain struggled to hold on to the water dispenser. "One of them tipped us with its fin," she shouted. "Get us stabilized, Commander!"

"As soon as I can, Captain," stuttered MacIntyre as he pulled himself across the furniture toward his control station. He flailed about, fighting dizziness and a churning stomach. Finally, he reached the controls. The ship stopped rolling.

"Hard to port — now!" ordered the captain.

The ship immediately banked left. At that moment, Lieutenant Ives staggered through the door, looking like he'd just gotten off a corkscrew roller coaster. "Does anyone have a barf bag?" he asked with a wobble in his voice.

"No time for that," barked the captain. "Get to your station. Dive!" she shouted. "Dive!"

"We're diving into a canyon," said the still-shaky Ives.

Just then about twenty little globular ships appeared, coming toward them like giant bubbles underwater. "Uh, put on your best smiles and spiff up your uniforms," said Captain Bruzelski. "We're about to have company."

"I'm trying to contact them," said Ives, "but they're not answering."

"Did you bang on the universal translator?" asked the captain.

"Aye, aye, sure did," said Ives.

"Here, I'll do it." She walked over and whacked the black box with her hand. "Ow!" She massaged her knuckles. "Why can't they make these things out of rubber?"

MacIntyre couldn't quite see what kind of creatures were piloting those little globes. For a moment, he thought he saw Kermit the Frog. "Nah, couldn't be," he said to himself. Then he saw a whole bunch of little blips on his sonar screen. "I'm picking up something scarier heading this way," he called out. "Torpedoes!" he shouted when he confirmed his suspicion. He pounded the alarm and heard the loud BLEE ... BLEE ... BLEE sound throughout the ship.

"They could have at least tried a hello. Get us out of here, Commander!" Captain Bruzelski shouted. "Punch it!"

Punch it he did as he spun the ship around. They sped through the undersea world like a supersonic whale.

"The torpedoes are still gaining on us!" the captain shouted. "Punch it again!"

MacIntyre felt the acceleration, but the torpedoes were still gaining on them like piranha on steroids.

4

Pink Wars

Those torpedo piranhas were closing fast. Another couple of heartbeats and the ship's tail would be blown to smithereens.

Being buried at sea had always sounded kind of heroic to Beamer, but that was in a blue sea, not a pink one ... and not until he had at least gotten past puberty.

At the last moment, the ship shot out of the pink ocean and kissed the sky. "We're free!" they all cried at once. The torpedoes leaped out of the water behind them, but having only propellers, they fell back into the sea.

As if they hadn't already had enough pink beneath the sea, they also faced a pink sky — a lighter shade, of course. Commander MacIntyre turned the ship to head toward what looked like a large island.

"Holy tamole! Even the land is pink!" said the captain.

She was sounding a little more like Scilla at the moment, thought MacIntyre. Hmm, who's Scilla? He couldn't quite place the name, but somehow he knew that she had always hated the color pink.

MacIntyre shook his head. Whoever Scilla was, she wouldn't like this planet. The dirt looked more pink than brown — a dark, orangish pink. Even the grass and brush were different shades of pink. A river wiggled through it all, also pink like the ocean. The least pinkish part of the landscape was a patch of land on either side of the river, which seemed to sparkle.

"How in blazes do things work on this planet?" asked Ives. "Usually, it's the chlorophyll in the green that soaks in sunlight for plants. Green doesn't seem to even exist here! Pink plants — what kind of chemical works in pink to pull in sunlight?"

"Let's have a closer look," said the captain. "Take us down, MacIntyre. Over there!"

It occurred to Beamer that they'd never "landed" the tree ship before. They'd crashed and been pulled in by a tractor beam, but never just ... landed. Luckily, Commander MacIntyre seemed to know what to do. It was weird having two minds in one head, but there were definite advantages in this case.

The ship hovered for a moment and then settled down on the pink-orange earth.

"The pink air seems to be breathable," announced Lieutenant Ives, "though a little lower than earth standard on oxygen." Then they stepped onto the alien world.

"The air smells like peppermint," said the captain in surprise.

MacIntyre ran to the water's edge and scanned it with his

analyzer. Then he cupped a handful and tasted it. "Like I figured, the river tastes like fruit punch. It's not salty like the sea." He happily slurped a few more handfuls. "It's sweet, very sweet."

"Captain, Commander, over here!" shouted the lieutenant from the edge of what had looked sparkly from above. "The trees ... their leaves are —"

"Glass!" said the captain as she walked toward the trees.

The glass leaves tinkled in the pink wind like wind chimes. They weren't totally transparent. Like everything else on this planet, the glass leaves were shades of pink.

"Yech, is that asparagus?" MacIntyre asked with a funny look, pointing toward a patch of plants nearby.

They were shaped like asparagus but colored purplish pink. MacIntyre picked one and sniffed it cautiously. He scanned it with his ... "thingamabob."

Beamer looked at the thingamabob through MacIntyre's eyes quizzically. He didn't remember seeing the tool before. It was one of those things that just happened to pop up on the ship when you needed it. He didn't even know what it was called. Commander MacIntyre probably knew it, though.

"This thing says that this asparagus stuff's safe to eat," the commander said.

Yeah, right, that's what they say about asparagus back home. Beamer had always wished that asparagus would get on the endangered-species list. He was sure it was only a matter of time before some terrorist figured out its potential for warfare. What better way to kill off the youth of America than by shoving asparagus down their throats?

Lieutenant Ives suddenly took the pink asparagus from MacIntyre and nibbled it. "Tastes like candy," he announced with a shrug. "Very sweet."

The lieutenant was definitely braver than MacIntyre had thought he was if he could chew a bite of asparagus without flinching. The commander reached for something that looked like peas in a pod, except, of course, the pod was pink. "Mmm," he muttered with his mouth full of peas. "They're kind of like M&M's. Everything tastes like candy here!" he shouted in pure joy.

Suddenly, small pink creatures that looked like babies with tiny wings began to flutter around them. "They're pink cherubs," said Captain Bruzelski. "You know, like you see flying around in old paintings or on wrapping paper for baby showers. Oh, they're so cute," she said as she reached up to tickle one of them.

Before the Star-Fighters could politely refuse, the little cherubs were serving them all kinds of candy plants, along with large cups filled with fruit punch from the river.

"Tastes like candy!" they repeated as they feasted on the different candy-flavored plants. Not too surprisingly, plants that looked like pink cotton turned out to taste like cotton candy.

Beamer noticed that for some reason they were all talking and acting more like their kid selves than their Star-Fighter characters.

A cherub with a crew cut scooped some pink mud into little cups for the Star-Fighters. It felt and tasted like soft-serve ice cream — peppermint flavored, of course.

MacIntyre turned to see Bruzelski take a bite of what looked like pink cauliflower.

Noticing that he was staring at her, Captain Bruzelski said, "Tastes like white chocolate. Honest."

The little cherubs began dancing wildly. Some appeared with heavy-metal band instruments and started playing while others danced.

Ives covered his ears and burped loudly. "What I wouldn't give for a french fry."

"What did you say, Ives?" asked MacIntyre, unable to hear anything above the band. "I don't suppose there are any rice and beans around here?" he asked as one of the creatures flew by. "I'm all sugared out."

"Me too," shouted the captain, who apparently had the best ears in the team. "I never thought I'd say this, but spinach is beginning to sound good to me."

"Yeah, I could even do with some okra," said MacIntyre. Yep, his sweet tooth was definitely getting worn out.

Little bumps began to appear on either side of those pink cherub heads, and their eyes started shifting up toward the top of their heads. All of a sudden, they looked more like Kermit the Frog than flying babies, except that these guys were definitely not as nice as Kermit.

As their pudgy little faces twisted into evil smiles, the creatures marched toward the Star-Fighters, tossing pink, candy-flavored items into their mouths like they were cherry bombs.

The Star-Fighters ducked and yelled for them to stop. The bombardment only got worse. MacIntyre finally stopped trying to say anything, since every time he opened his mouth, he'd get a mouthful of candy. That strategy was flawed, however, by the fact that when he didn't open his mouth, his face and uniform would get another coat of gooey or sticky morsels.

"Back to the ship!" the captain shouted as she ducked under a barrage of cauliflower. The little bumps on those cherub heads had now become full-fledged devil horns! They were goblins, not cherubs, and were tossing candy veggies like machine-gun fire at the fleeing Star-Fighters.

5

Mission Abort!

The Star-Fighters were so stuffed that they were chugging more than running. They ducked to evade candy potatoes, celery, and artichokes. By the time they got to the ship, their uniforms were a sticky, candy-coated mess.

Lieutenant Ives pelted one goblin with cans of sauerkraut from their food rations after the goblin lobbed some candy squash at him.

The captain, meanwhile, battled another goblin who was tossing candy lettuce and broccoli at her. She finally took a broom and swatted it out the door. "Hit the thrusters!" she cried when she finally secured the door.

The little goblins, now numbering in the hundreds, continued to bombard the ship with sugary vegetables.

"Hey, that stuff is eating through the hull!" yelled Ives.

"Lieutenant, activate the stickeyon matter gummerupper — now!" the captain shouted.

For once, they seemed to have the right weapon. Something like a shock wave bolted from the ship, and the goblins suddenly looked like they were wrapped in bubble gum.

Meanwhile, Commander MacIntyre wiped the candy muck off his fingers and again punched the engines. They zoomed into the pink sky and sighed in relief as the pink planet shrank behind them into the black cosmos.

Feeling very stuffed from the sugar attack, Ives tried to stifle a belch. It didn't work. His burp created a world-class atmospheric disturbance. That was because not only Ives, but MacIntyre and Bruzelski as well, belched at the same time.

They were lucky the ship didn't blow up. As it was, the ship bounced back into the tree, the windows burst open, and most of Murphy Street was gassed with something that smelled like sour peppermint.

Luckily, when their uniforms dissolved back to their everyday clothes, the candy muck dissolved with them. Beamer couldn't imagine how he would explain being candy coated to his parents. He had a feeling it was going to take a while for the peppermint smell to fade, though.

*   *   *   *   *

That night, Beamer couldn't eat the pink Jell-O ring his mother made for dessert. She looked puzzled. After all, he'd always liked it before. The next morning, when his sister came into the breakfast room wearing not only her pink Nikes but also pink jeans, Beamer couldn't handle it. He ran from the table and skidded into the bathroom. What happened next is up to your imagination. Hopefully you're not reading this during dinner.

Beamer was relieved when he was finally on his way to school, but he stopped halfway down the street.

"What's the matter?" Scilla asked, with Michael acting as her echo.

"Well, there's way too much pink in my life," Beamer said, "and I've got a feeling it's because of the girl in the Pink Palace."

That's when Scilla noticed that they were standing in front of the girl's house. "Oh, no, you don't," she said. "I got a glimpse of her in that picture. She's a girl—a real girl who wears frilly dresses and probably primps, giggles, and talks about her hair all day."

"Come on, Scilla," Beamer argued. "You're as much of a girl as she is, whether you want to admit it or not, and if she needs help—"

"Not a chance. There are girls, and there are girls. That subspecies of *Homo sapiens girlus* has always given me a lot of trouble, so if you want to help her, you'll have to do it without me." With that she whirled around and stomped on down the street.

"Scillaaaaa!" Beamer called after her. He heaved a huge sigh and stumbled on toward school.

*   *   *   *   *

For the next three days, Scilla angled her nose at two o'clock and walked to school by herself. Ghoulie set up dentist appointments and extra-credit P.E. assignments for himself. Since Ghoulie hated both dentists and P.E., Beamer figured he hated Beamer's crazy idea even more. For that matter, the last thing on planet Earth that Beamer wanted to do was to ask some girl to come out and play. So, for the time being, all rescue operations connected to the color pink were strictly "no go." It didn't take long for things to change, though.

Beamer was in the school cafeteria trying to decide if his meatball lunch would make a good weapon of mass destruction when Scilla and Ghoulie suddenly appeared across the table. Neither of them looked well. Their hair was all scraggly, and they had dark shadows around their eyes.

"We've been cursed," said Scilla.

"Not cursed," said Ghoulie, rolling his eyes, "just psychologically dissociated due to residual guilt-driven stimuli in the hippocampus."

"What's that supposed to mean?" asked Beamer, shaking his head in bewilderment.

"Well the hippocampus is the region of the brain which—"

"We've been having pink dreams," Scilla said, interrupting him. "Three straight nights of them. One thing's for sure," she added, "I hate anything pink and sweet so much now that I'll probably be having fewer cavities for a while."

"Yeah," said Ghoulie. "Those pudgy little pink cherubs we met on the planet have gotten into our heads."

"Cherubs ... nothing!" said Scilla. "They were goblins, plain and simple. We've gotta do somethin' about that girl before we all go crazy!"

"What the heck are you talking about?" asked Ghoulie. "We don't even know if there's anything wrong with her! I'll put my money on going back to the pink planet and blowing it up!"

"Somehow, I don't think blowing things up is what the Star-Fighters are all about," Beamer said with a put-down grimace. Of course, he liked shooting up things as well as the next guy. In video games, you could be a hero or a bad guy with no pain and no guilt. You just had to keep from thinking about the fact that real shooting was all about pain and guilt without the advantage of extra lives.

"Things happen to us for a reason," Beamer insisted, "at least things connected with the tree ship. Remember when we almost crashed on the space platform?"

"Yeah, so what?" Ghoulie answered.

"Well, right after that we met Solomon Parker, whose whole life was a wreck, with broken inventions and abandoned projects everywhere around him."

"So you're thinking all these pink attacks, dream-wise or otherwise, have something to do with that girl in the pink house," Ghoulie grumbled, regretting the words as he said them.

"You're right, though," Beamer said, looking at Ghoulie. "We've got no idea what's goin' on with this girl. I mean, is she locked in and made to scrub floors like Cinderella?"

"For all we know," Scilla chimed in, "she may be allergic to everything and has to live in a glass bubble."

"Or maybe exposure to the smog-infested atmosphere has changed her into a drooling, bloodsucking, pink octopus," said Ghoulie, dipping into his taste for Saturday-night 1950s horror reruns.

6

First Contact

Scilla was in a mood to spit nails. They'd watched the girl's house for a week without seeing her come out once. They'd seen the lady with the pointed nose and a tall, dark-haired man going and coming, but no girl. So Scilla had been elected to go to the girl's front door and ask if she wanted to play.

Holy tamole! thought Scilla. *The fact that I'm a girl has nothing to do with why I'm the one who has to knock on the door of the pink castle. Beamer and Ghoulie are just like the cowardly lion when it comes to girls. Of course, they didn't think of me as being a girl.* That was sort of good and sort of not, although she wasn't exactly sure why. *The frilly girl will probably want to play hopscotch or dress-up or do something with paper dolls. She might even try to steal her mother's makeup and give me lips the size of a billboard. This is crazy! They even talked me into wearing a dress! Talk about humiliation. If it weren't for those stupid pink dreams—drat it all!*

Scilla huddled up tight next to the gate, hoping no one would see her in a dress. Beamer and Ghoulie were standing back a few feet, snickering. Scilla gave them a searing look and pushed the call button.

A few seconds later, somebody answered, "Hello, may I *ahsk* who is calling?" Scilla recognized the voice of the woman with the pointed nose.

"My name is Scilla Bruzelski and I was wondering—"

"Yes, Ms. Bruzelski," the voice interrupted her, "and what is *yoah* business?"

"I just wanted to see if … uh … your little girl could come out and play?"

"What?" the voice said as if Scilla had asked for the family jewels. "How did you know a little *gahl* lived *heah*?"

"Well, I was here the other day when Beamer—that's Beamer MacIntyre—dropped off some papers from school for her."

"Oh, yes, I see. Uh … she doesn't play … uh … outside—"

"Then can I come inside and play with her?" Scilla asked, feeling like she was making the ultimate sacrifice.

"Uh … no. She doesn't play. I mean, she isn't allowed to play with *strangahs*—with anyone." The woman sounded a little rattled as she went on. "You see … uh … she's … uh—I mean, she's a special child and … uh … not allowed to play with anyone."

Good grief, Scilla thought, *I've never heard so many "uh's" coming from an adult before. This lady definitely has something to hide.*

"Thank you for *yoah consahn*," the voice continued, "but please don't call again. She can't, you see. She just can't." There was something funny about the way her voice sounded. It was almost like she was ready to cry.

Scilla heard a *click*, and the speaker was silent. "Well, that's that," she said as she turned to Ghoulie and Beamer. She was so relieved she didn't have to play with the girl, she almost felt like dancing the jig—except, of course, she didn't know how to dance the jig.

"Sounds an awful lot like what we heard when we tried to visit Solomon Parker," said Beamer.

"Yeah, sure does," echoed Ghoulie.

At that moment, the mail carrier walked by and started to slip a large bundle of mail into the mailbox. It didn't fit in the box very well, and several envelopes and pieces of junk mail fell to the ground. Scilla picked them up and handed them back to the mail carrier. She got a "thank you" in return and something else—she'd seen the name Malcolm Franck on three of the envelopes.

*　*　*　*　*

Ghoulie didn't look all that amazed when he actually found something about a person named Malcolm Franck on the Internet. But then, outside of the CIA and the NSA, Ghoulie and his computer had the best chance of tracking anyone down.

Scilla had never seen Ghoulie's place, and she was wide-eyed when she finally did. His town house looked like something out of the *Jetsons*. There were glass walls that could be either see-through or not at the push of a button. Scilla didn't see any robotic maids running about, but somebody or something spent a lot of time pumping Windex on all the glass. In fact, everything looked so shiny and clean, she was almost afraid to breathe on, let alone touch, anything. She wondered how real people could actually live here.

But then Ghoulie took them up three floors in a cylindrical glass elevator to his room. Scilla's eyes popped open even wider.

Ghoulie's room was about the size of an entire floor in her grandma's house! It was divided into three different sections. One part was for music and TV and gave a whole new meaning to the idea of "home theater." Another part was for jumping and climbing and bouncing around, complete with a trampoline, jungle gym, pogo stick, and a whole maze system to climb, crawl, slide, or jump through. Still another section was set off for electronics and radio-controlled cars, trains, planes, and boats. It wasn't up there with Solomon Parker's automated world, but then you could only get so much into a town house without scaring the neighbors.

This is ridiculous. No kid should be allowed to have this much stuff! It was un-American. It was disgusting: anything he wanted, Ghoulie's parents got for him. In fact, there was a good chance they didn't wait for him to ask. Of course, the reason they got him all this stuff was because they were rarely at home. Pretty good deal, you'd think—everything in the world to play with and no parents around to tell you what you couldn't do all the time. She wondered if Ghoulie looked at it that way.

When she finally made it up to his computer loft, Scilla saw computers of every size and shape, along with just about anything that could be attached to a computer, including some parts that only the Department of Defense might recognize.

Before she could take a good breath, Ghoulie was already online and searching sites with language so technical, Scilla had a better chance of reading Sanskrit. They found the name Malcolm Franck on the website for a major chemical company. He was identified as a scientist who had developed a new kind of insecticide. There was only so much a seventh-grade brain could process, no matter how smart it was, but they knew the word *genetics.* Apparently, Franck had genetically engineered his insecticide to target certain insects without harming other insects, animals, plants, or human beings. The company billed it as being quite a breakthrough—up there with the invention of the electric lightbulb.

Dr. Franck's discovery had made him mucho rich, but it had come at a price. His wife had worked for the same company but had been killed in a toxic chemical spill four years ago.

"There's nothing here about their daughter, though," said Ghoulie.

Since the lady on the call speaker had mentioned that she was "special," Scilla suggested he try hitting hospitals and clinics to look for records about her. He found no records at all!

"It's beginning to sound more and more like Solomon Parker all over again," grumbled Beamer.

"Could be," Scilla said, "but the lady doesn't sound like Mrs. Drummond."

"You can't tell from her voice," said Beamer. "Some people have a special voice to talk with visitors and another one for every day. Remember how greasy-sweet Cinderella's stepmother sounded at the ball?"

"That's a fairy tale, MacIntyre," Ghoulie said with a wry grin.

"Oh, she's hiding something, though" said Scilla. "I'm sure of that."

7

Invasion

It was D-day, or Pink Day ... whatever. They were going to invade the Pink Palace! The Star-Fighters had waited until the lady with the pointed nose was out of the house and the father was still at work. All systems were go! They were going to use pretty much the same procedure that had gotten them to Solomon Parker. Hopefully, the Pink Palace wouldn't have as big a yard or be guarded by robots that looked like giant daddy longlegs.

Of course, they couldn't climb all the backyard fences and walls between Beamer's house and the Pink Palace, and they couldn't just drop into her backyard with parachutes. That left the old "me Tarzan, you Jane" transportation system—through the trees. There wouldn't be any swinging, though. They had discovered secret passages through the trees. You see, somebody or something had broken or trimmed back tree branches to form arch-ways through which people could walk. These arched tun-nels went from tree to tree all over the neighborhood. It wasn't as if Murphy Street didn't have enough mys-teries. This one, though, was really weird. Secret passages were supposed to be in old houses and underground, not in the treetops.

"Have you checked to see if one of these passages goes through our tree?" asked Ghoulie.

Beamer's face stretched into a sheepish expression. "Come to think of it, I guess I haven't."

"Holy tamole!" said Scilla. "Do we even know if one happens to cross over her yard?"

"We'll just have to take our chances," said Beamer. "If it doesn't, we may have to make a little detour to get there. Come on," he said. "Let's start lookin' in our tree. Spread out. Remember these things aren't all that easy to spot unless you happen into them."

The tree was filled with the sound of swishing and creaking branches as they each took a different route up through the branches. Then it happened like magic. One moment Scilla was removing a twig that had snapped into her face, and the next she ducked down and around to see the passage rotate into view, front and center. It was like she'd suddenly switched from a 2-D to a 3-D world. "Whoa!" she said. "Hey, y'all, I found it!" she shouted to the others.

The first time they were in one of these tree tunnels, it had been winter. Now, with leaves starting to pop out all along the way, it looked like the passage had green wallpaper. Magical and fanciful is how Scilla thought of it, like something out of a fairy tale. "There it is," she said when Beamer and Ghoulie joined her. "Not exactly straight and true, but mostly running along the same direction as Murphy Street."

"Which means it will probably cross the backyard of the girl's house," said Beamer.

Scilla had the sense they were walking in one of those hedge mazes. With the sunlight shooting between the leaves, it was very bright, almost like walking in the sky. That's not to say it wasn't scary. After all, the branches below their feet weren't all that close together. Every once in a while, she lost her footing and fell through. There were plenty of handholds, though, so she always caught herself — at the cost of a few scrapes and scratches. Scilla planned to wear long sleeves next time — maybe even a jean jacket.

Finally, they came to a yard that reeked of pink. The house — three stories tall plus an attic — looked even more like a pink birthday cake from the higher angle. Feeling a touch of nausea coming on at the thought, she shifted her gaze to the backyard. Smaller pink items were scattered about — a swing, a wishing well, several park benches, a gazebo, even a pink jungle gym.

The biggest pink thing, other than the house itself, was a playhouse shaped like a castle. Complete with delicate towers, it was perched atop a man-made hill with steps that wound around, leading up to the pink castle gate. Circular stairs in the back led to a second story and up to a tower.

She must be a little "princess." Scilla rolled her eyes at the thought. She had run up against them before. *Anything they wanted, they'd get, and everything had to be perfect — perfect hair, perfect eyes, and perfect face. They didn't wear clothes; they wore costumes. This little party was going to be a nightmare!*

She suddenly saw a pair of eyes staring up at them from a tower window. "Hey, y'all —" she called.

They heard a scream and saw a girl hurriedly trample around the staircase, out the gate, and down around the winding steps. Scilla rolled her eyes and sighed when she saw the pink dress with all the ruffles.

"Hey, wait! / Hey, stop! / We come in peace!" Beamer, Scilla, and Ghoulie yelled at the same time as the pink girl ran into the house.

So much for the damsel-in-distress idea. At the moment, they were the ones causing her distress. Without thinking the situation through, they quickly rustled down the tree, dropped to the ground, and ran after her. They scrambled up a broad set of steps onto a stone patio as wide as the house. Then they shot through a wide set of glass doors and down a broad hallway.

Before they could skid to a stop, they were in a room right out of Disneyland. The whole front wall was curved and had a row of fancy windows about four times as tall as Scilla. These had half-circle windows at the top with lots of squiggly designs. Chairs, sofas, cabinets, grandfather and mantel clocks, lamps, and bookcases were all delicately designed in shades of pink with lots of curves and squiggles like they'd come out of *Beauty and the Beast* or *Aladdin*. Some people probably would have called it pretty, but after a few pink dreams and a trip to a pink planet, Scilla just found it sickly sweet. It made her dizzy just looking at them. What she would have given for a few straight lines.

Everything that wasn't pink was made of glass. Hundreds of little glass dolphins or unicorns or dragons ... whatever ... covered the tables and filled the cabinets. They reflected the light coming through the windows, casting sparkles around the walls and ceiling like a mirror ball at a dance party. Strangely enough, though, Scilla noticed that you couldn't see a ghost of a reflection in the larger pieces of glass—the glass cases or the windows.

Everything looked so ... breakable that she was afraid to move. Scilla slapped Ghoulie's hand away when he tried to touch the horn of a glass unicorn. But she accidentally knocked off a glass penguin. In the process of trying to catch that, they tipped over still more glass figures. It was like a chain reaction! Before they knew it, they had a full-scale glass avalanche. All three of them ended up doing a major juggling act that involved several incredible jumps and diving catches. Amazingly, nothing was broken, but they were left lying on the floor, sucking their breath in like they'd just come up from a deep-sea dive without diving suits.

There was no sign of the girl, however. Scilla was relieved that she had, at least, stopped screaming.

Ghoulie was the first one to finally ask the obvious. "Uh ... guys, what if she called 9–1–1?"

"Yeah, a life of crime isn't what I had in mind," Beamer said.

"I don't know. I think she's hiding," Scilla said as she opened a door. The room behind the door turned out to be a very fancy bathroom—pink, of course, but with gold fixtures, knobs, and holders. "Hey, there's no mirror in the bathroom," she called out. "At least *something* about the place isn't perfect."

"Come on, let's get out of here," Beamer said. He started to run out but suddenly stopped and stared at something hanging above a big fireplace.

Scilla came over for a look. The fireplace was made of pink stones and had a pink marble mantel. What Beamer was staring at, though, was a large painting of a woman. Nobody probably would have noticed it there in the shadow of the staircase, if it hadn't been lit by several spotlights. Looking at the lady in the dark, cloudy background gave Scilla a particularly eerie feeling. She heard a girl's voice and whirled around.

"Who are you, and what do you want?" the girl asked from atop a winding staircase.

She stood with her head and shoulders in shadow. Beamer walked toward the steps saying, "We're just kids from down the street. We thought . . . uh—"

"We thought you might want someone to play with," Scilla said when she heard Beamer hesitate.

"You want to play with me?" the girl said as she stepped toward them into the light. They recoiled from her as if she were a snake about to strike.

8

The Good, the Bad, and the Ugly

She was very feminine, as Scilla had said she would be. Her blonde hair and clothes were as beautiful as you'd find on a fairy princess. But her face ... her face was all wrong! She was, in fact—Beamer hated to use the word—*ugly*! The Wicked Witch of the West had better skin tones! Even the Mummy would have winced at the sight of her. Her skin was as white as a ghost and she looked ... old! She could rival Old Lady Parker in the wrinkle department, but then Ms. Parker was ninety-three years old and lived in a house that looked like a transplant from Transylvania.

The girl's twisted face took on what Beamer guessed was a puzzled look. "What's the matter?" she asked. "You don't need to worry. I didn't call the police—not after I saw that you were kids."

He swallowed hard, noticing that Ghoulie and Scilla were doing the same. "We didn't mean to scare you," he said through a windpipe squeezed so tight he could hardly push his voice through it. "We're just not used to someone who looks like—" He suddenly stopped himself, remembering the missing mirrors. *Yes, the windows and glass panels. They were nonreflective! She didn't know what she looked like!*

"He means," Scilla finished for him, "we're not used to seeing anyone dressed like a princess. We just wondered if you'd like to ... play."

"I'm not allowed to play with anyone," the girl said, like it was one of the Ten Commandments. "My father says that the outside world and the people living in it are dangerous and ... and evil." She paused nervously a moment then asked, "Are you ... evil?"

"Uh ... no," Beamer said. "We're just kids." Actually, at the back of his mind the same question had been haunting him about her. *Was she evil? She looked like it. You could always tell evil by how ugly it looked. An evil witch had twisted features; an evil creature had ugly tentacles or twisted limbs; an evil tree had twisted branches.*

At the moment, none of them seemed to know what to do. The impulse to run away was strong, but there was something about the girl that made Beamer unwilling to do that. She seemed so delicate and innocent, like she might break with the wrong word or look.

Do evil people have feelings? "I mean, there are bad people out there," Beamer said out loud to her. "But most people wouldn't think of hurting anyone. At least that's what my mom and dad say." It occurred to him that his parents probably hadn't been to a school playground lately. *Jared is not the only bully in middle school.*

"You have a mother?" the girl asked.

"Yes, of course," Beamer answered with a shrug.

"Mine's dead," the girl said with almost no feeling. "That's her," she said, pointing toward the large portrait above the fireplace, "in the picture."

Beamer was shamefaced at having said something so ignorant. Of course, some people didn't have a mother or a father. His friend Jack didn't have a father; neither did Scilla. Some didn't have either one.

"She's very pretty," Scilla said, looking at the portrait.

Beamer looked from the painting to the girl. *She looked nothing like her mother, except for the hair color . . . and maybe the eyes. If the woman in the picture was truly her mother, then something must have gone terribly wrong for this little girl.*

"My dad said she was smarter and prettier than any woman in the whole world. He told me I would probably be pretty and smart too." She seemed at a loss for words after saying that. Finally, she said, "Yes, I would like someone to play with . . . if you are sure that you are not evil."

Just then they heard a car rumbling up the driveway.

"Oh, no, that's my nanny, Ms. Warrington!" the girl cried. "She can't see you here! You must go . . . quickly!"

They sprinted back the way they had come in.

"No, not that way," she yelled at them. "She'll see you in the backyard. This way! Hurry!" She motioned for them to come up the stairs toward her.

With only a moment's hesitation, and after taking a deep breath, they scrambled up the steps. Before they got too unbearably close to that distorted face, however, she swung about and ran down a wide hallway. Since straight lines were apparently frowned on by whoever built this house, the hallway was curved.

"Alana, I'm home," they heard a voice downstairs call out. "You can come out now. The housekeeper has finished cleaning up." Her voice suddenly changed. "That's strange. She didn't do as good a job as usual—"

Beamer skipped up the steps as fast as he could without running over the girl. *So her name is Alana.* Somehow the name didn't seem to fit the face.

Alana led them up another flight of stairs and into another hallway, which ended in front of a large window. She opened it to reveal a small balcony overlooking the backyard. "This way," she said.

They all blinked rapidly or rubbed their eyes as they passed her, trying to avoid looking directly at her. A large branch from the tree overhung the balcony.

"Since that's the way you came, I guess that's the way you want to leave," she said. "And ... and when you come back, if I'm not in the yard, you can come in this way. This window is never locked, and I am always here. But you must never come when anyone else is here."

"How are we to know—?"

"Daddy has a flag on the roof. I'll put a little flag under it when it's clear. Okay?"

"Yeah ... sure," Beamer said awkwardly. It was a pretty safe bet that none of them ever wanted to come back, but what could he say?

"We'll keep a lookout," Scilla said as she hoisted herself onto the branch. "Bye."

"Uh ... right ... sure thing!" Ghoulie said, avoiding her gaze.

The Star-Fighters said almost nothing to each other all the way back to the tree ship. Beamer had no idea what to do. *How do you help somebody like her?* They had no healing powers that they knew of. Sure, Solomon seemed to be healthier after his trip in the tree ship, but that wasn't the main thing that had happened. He mainly rediscovered who he really was and found a sense of God's purpose in his life. But if you were going to heal someone's body, why would you need to go on an elaborate fantasy? Nothing about this job with the girl made any sense!

* * * * *

At school the next day, Scilla banged down her pencil on her desk and heaved a big sigh. *I hate coordinates—x equals this, and y equals that. Coordinates make sense when I'm the captain of the tree ship, but in the classroom it's a major bore.* She looked over her shoulder at the clock on the back wall. *Holy tamole, it's almost four o'clock! I'm never gonna get out of here.*

"What's the matter, Scilla?" asked her teacher at the front of the room. "You can do this. I know you can."

Yep, you guessed it. Scilla had been kept after school for extra study. Her grades had been falling in spite of the fact that she was in a program for gifted kids. The trouble was, Scilla didn't feel gifted. Why did they keep insisting that she was? All she wanted was to be left alone. *Okay, so my grades aren't stellar. What's the big deal? If I don't care, why should they?*

Her brother was the gifted one. He was actually only her half brother. That's because, soon after Scilla was born, her mother had married someone who was not Scilla's father. Less than a year later, her brother was born. Her stepfather didn't want her living with them, which is why she ended up living with her grandmother. Sometimes, when things weren't going all that well and she was feeling sad already, she'd cry about being kept away from her mother. But the next day, she'd be the toughest girl in her class and ready to wrestle anyone—boy or girl—to the ground if they crossed her.

It was funny that she was thinking of her brother just now.

There were times when Scilla thought she had a "sixth sense." That afternoon proved to be one of those times.

* * * * *

"Hey, big sister, why ya' comin' home so late?"

Yep, it was Scilla's stepbrother, Dashiell. He had come to visit their grandmother. Scilla groaned. She always seemed to come out on the losing side whenever he was around. Compared to her, he was Mr. Perfect—well-groomed, well-dressed, perfectly polite, athletic, and very good-looking. Oh, and she forgot something else: he was a "gifted" kid in a whole school for gifted kids. Her mother was very proud of him. So was her grandma. Scilla wished she could disappear through a mirror or down a rabbit hole.

"Too bad you're not out for spring vacation yet," Dashiell said with a mock look of sympathy. "But then I guess that's not the reason you're home late." He chuckled and left the room.

Scilla dropped her backpack and crumpled to the floor. He didn't like her any more than his father did. But she really wanted him to like her. *Things always seem to go wrong for me when Dashiell is around.*

That's exactly what happened—right in the middle of that thought. Her grandmother's parakeet suddenly fluttered into the room. *How did he get out of his cage?*

Dashiell suddenly ran back into the room, putting a light jacket on as he headed to the front door. "I think I'll go outside and play while you're doing your homework." He flung the door open and stood in the doorway fumbling with his jacket.

If Huckleberry gets out the door, he'll be gone for sure! "Close the door!" she screamed as she leaped around trying to catch the parakeet. *Grandma will be totally sick if she loses this bird.*

"Huh?" Dashiell said with an innocent look.

"Dashiell … the door!" Scilla cried again. Scilla finally caught the bird on its glide path toward the door, tripping over a coffee table and falling face-first to the floor in the process. While she was catching her breath, her grandmother's black shoe buckle suddenly loomed directly in front of her eyes. "Uh-oh," she said with a gulp.

9

Moon Child

"Scilla!" her grandmother exclaimed. "What are you doing with Huckleberry?"

Scilla tilted her head slowly upward, scanned up the green flower-patterned dress, past the black velvet belt and the lace collar to the scowl on her grandma's face. "He got out of his cage," Scilla said as she got back to her feet while still holding the bird in both hands.

"Yes, she saved it from getting out the door," Dashiell said.

For a brief moment Scilla felt good.

But then Dashiell went on, "Of course, it would have been better if she hadn't let it out of the cage in the first place. I didn't actually see her do it, but you know how she likes to show off when I'm around."

"Scilla!" her grandma said through a tight jaw with her fists on her hips. "Put Huckleberry back in his cage and get up to your room right now!"

"But—" Scilla started.

"You know better than to play with Huckleberry out of his cage," her grandmother added. "Just because your brother is visiting, it's no time to take leave of your senses."

Scilla felt like melting into the floor. There was no sense arguing about it. She'd fed him in the morning. Maybe she'd left the cage door unlocked.

* * * * *

Scilla didn't have to stay late after school the next day, but she wished she had. She hurried in the house to drop off her backpack and change her clothes, as usual. But then Dashiell glided into her room and insisted on telling her the words he'd spelled to win fifteen spelling bees in a row. It was like listening to a talking dictionary. He kept spitting out words until she started seeing them flittering about the room like moths.

When he finished, she started to move toward the door, but then he had to tell her about their grandma's tea party earlier that day. He told her how silly the old ladies looked and talked — how Mrs. Jacobs kept pulling up her knee-high nylons, and how Mrs. Hedley tapped on her hearing aid and yelled, "What was that?" after anyone said anything.

Still, he'd apparently been a hit. Oh yeah, he had schmoozing down to a science. With his perfect looks and charm, he probably had his grandma and the other ladies thinking he was an up-and-coming Cary Grant.

Scilla finally thumped down the stairs two at a time with him scrambling after her. But before she could get out the door, he said he had a surprise for her. He pointed to an end table across the living room. Sure enough, a chocolate bar lay on top. That was about the only candy she could still stomach eating these days. *Wow! Maybe he liked her after all.*

"Thank you," she said, giving him a big smile and walking

over to the table. She picked up the candy and started back toward him. Half a second later, her grandma's crystal lamp spun off the table. She didn't notice that she had hit it, but she saw it crash to smithereens on the floor. "Eeeeiiii!" Scilla yelped in a squeak dripping with panic. "No! This is Grandma's favorite lamp!" She was totally worm meat now—maybe even pond scum.

With trembling hands, and aching with anguish in about every part of her body, Scilla cleaned up the broken crystals and retrieved the tasseled shade and marble base. In the process, she found a long thread so thin and clear that it was almost invisible. It was fishing line. She remembered it from the time her uncle Ted had taken her fishing. Maybe Grandma had used it to fix something. Wiping tears from her eyes, she put everything in a large bowl—just in case the lamp could be fixed—and ran crying out the door.

Scilla knew that she would probably be grounded again—for good reason, she admitted. She wiped away the last of the tears with her shirtsleeve and started climbing up to the tree ship. To get to the tree, she didn't have to go into Beamer's yard. His big tree had a split trunk. One half went almost straight up. The other half ran up at about the angle of a playground slide, crossing over into her yard before it turned to a more vertical rise. All she had to do was hoist herself up and crab-walk up to where she could hop onto a branch that took a diagonal course toward the tree ship.

She almost forgot how depressed she was when she smelled the honeysuckle and hibiscus flowers. Right there, about halfway up the angled trunk, Scilla decided to make this day—her last day before being grounded—a great one. Suddenly she was no longer plodding up the tree, but practically dancing. Some of her grandma's red bougainvillea had wound itself into the tree. Nothing was better than the colors and smells of spring. Best of all, though, were the bright green leaves that waved to her an enthusiastic greeting in the breeze. A gentle cloud of spinning white dandelion seeds also glided by, each sparkling in the evening sunlight. For a moment, she felt like she was in a fairyland where nothing could possibly go wrong.

Just as she plopped down on the wooden platform next to the tree ship's door, she saw a patch of pink flapping in the distance. She pulled some branches back for a better look and then gave a heavy sigh—one with a little "eek" in it.

* * * * *

A few minutes later, the elevator creaked to a halt next to the ship. Beamer and Ghoulie locked the elevator into place, tossed a few yellow-white kernels of popcorn into their mouths, and turned toward the ship. Scilla was sitting, hunched down next to the door, elbows on knees, chin in hands, looking like she was awaiting the end of the world.

"Hey, what's up?" Beamer asked her as he crunched his popcorn.

She pivoted her head sideways on her hand. "Look for yourself—that away," she said, cocking a thumb northward, up the street.

Beamer and Ghoulie stopped crunching at the same time and stared. Beamer handed the bowl to Ghoulie and crossed over to push away the branches. Yep, sure enough, there it was—a flag—a pink flag—waving on the roof of Alana's house. Talk about kicking the joy out of the day; even the leaves seemed to sag.

Beamer sank down next to Scilla. "Now what do we do?" he asked morosely.

"I don't think we have much choice," groaned Scilla. "We promised!"

"Hey, we didn't say the word *promise*, did we?" Ghoulie argued. But then he saw the look on their faces. "Okay, okay, so we gave her the idea we'd be back. Uh ... maybe we can keep our promise later," he said as he sat cross-legged facing them. He tossed a popcorn kernel into the air, caught it on his tongue, and snapped it into his mouth like a frog catching a fly.

"You know what'll happen if we don't visit her," grumbled Scilla.

"Oh, right," said Ghoulie with a wince, "I almost forgot—more pink dreams."

"Well, we might as well get this over with," said Beamer as he stood up.

Beamer launched up to the nearest branch. "One thing we gotta figure out on the way over," he said, "is how to play without staring at her face all the time."

"Yeah, she'll suspect something is wrong if we keep doin' that," Scilla agreed. Now that she was more familiar with the route, she skipped from branch to branch like a tree fairy—light as a feather.

"Probably the best approach," said Ghoulie, "would be to concentrate on what we're doing and look at her only when we have to."

"She'll notice if we avoid looking at her," said Scilla, shaking her head.

"Then we'd better come up with a picture in our heads that we can substitute for her real face," Beamer said as he lofted himself up into the corridor they would travel through the trees.

*   *   *   *   *

Alana heard them land on the balcony and rushed to greet them. Right away they practiced looking straight at her and smiling while imagining somebody else's face. Beamer used the face of Lisa from the *Simpsons*—well, they were both blonde, anyway.

One thing was for sure—Alana was no Cinderella. Her room was actually three rooms—a bedroom, a bathroom, and a huge playroom. It wasn't as big as Ghoulie's play-room, but it had everything a girl could want—dolls and stuffed animals, books, art supplies, a computer, more glass figures—kept out of harm's way—and a mini carousel.

Luckily, she also had a few things guys liked to mess around with. Ghoulie had a lot more fun than he had expected—playing with cars, big and small, that scooted around, vrooming and honking on the floor, and planes that would fly around the room sounding like tiny lawn mow-ers. The trouble, of course, was that even these were mostly colored pink. Beamer swallowed hard each time he touched one of them.

As far as he could tell, Alana seemed to be having a good time. If anything, she seemed a little hyperexcited to have people to play with. There were a few times when she had trouble sharing. Beamer was about to chalk this trait up to her "evil" side, when it occurred to him that she probably hadn't had much practice. *How do you learn to share when you have no one to share with?*

Yeah, this girl might as well have been born on the moon. Planet Earth was a total mystery to her. She had no TV and no video-game machine. She did have a computer, which Ghoulie hooked on to right away. But it had no connection to the Internet. The only programs on the machine were educational ones.

That's not to say Alana wasn't smart. When it came to

facts, she was a walking, talking encyclopedia. All they had to do was say a word—like maybe *albatross*—and she'd rattle off what it meant in incredible detail.

She was no slouch when it came to numbers either. Ghoulie was on her computer, trying to show her where he lived, when she popped down beside him and used her map and geography programs to calculate the distance to his house, how far the house was from the exact center of the city, and the pollution content of the air around his house. All Ghoulie could do was gulp.

To Beamer, it seemed she was more like a robot in the process of being programmed than a kid learning. It was weird. There were huge gaps in her "programming."

The more he thought about it, the more worried Beamer became. You couldn't tell by looking—what with her having a big house full of goodies—but, no doubt about it, Alana lived in a bubble. Whatever else she might be, she was every bit as delicate as one of her glass figurines. Any moment, he worried, they could accidentally do or say something that would break her and her bubble into a thousand pieces.

10
Oh, Brother

It wasn't surprising that Alana wanted to know everything about everything outside her bubble. Some of her questions were kind of strange.

"How can you walk to school?" she asked Scilla. "Won't the gangs kill you before you get there?"

What she did know about the world was definitely a little warped.

"Well, I've heard about gangs," Scilla said, "but I've never seen any around here—except for the Scull Cross gang. They're mean, but they don't kill anyone."

"But aren't there wars and plagues and criminals and hypocrites everywhere?" Alana asked.

"I haven't seen any of that stuff either," said Scilla with a shrug, "except on TV. Well, I might have seen a hypocrite, I suppose, since I don't know what that is."

Beamer looked questioningly at Ghoulie, who merely shrugged and said, "Me neither. I guess that's something you learn after the seventh grade."

"I think ... well, I mean you're thinking about it all wrong," Beamer said. "Bad things do happen, but an awful lot of good things happen too—much more than the bad, maybe. And if you spend your time worrying about the bad things, you never see the good things." He'd said something like that to his mom when they were watching the fireflies one night last summer. She thought it sounded pretty good.

Alana tilted her head sideways to think about it. *Good* and *bad*—did Alana even know what the words meant? Beamer wondered.

Beamer tried to see Alana as she really was. In fact, the more he looked at her, the less ugly she seemed. Once, they were both driving electric cars when they bumped head-on into each other. Beamer got a close look at her face. She definitely had the face of an old woman—a very old woman, like the old crone Snow White's stepmother turned into to give her the poisoned apple. He couldn't help taking a deep gulp.

Then it happened—the moment of doom Beamer had been afraid of.

"Do you think I'm pretty?" he heard Alana ask Scilla.

It was like Murphy Street had suddenly become Hiroshima. He was choking and coughing like he was in the middle of the mushroom cloud.

Scilla was turning pink—or was it green? She cleared her throat nervously, hemming and hawing. If she didn't think of something to say soon, she would probably shrivel up from the fallout.

"Not that I'd be as pretty as you are, of course," Alana added before Scilla could say anything.

Beamer could tell from Scilla's expression that, however much she had come to like Alana before, she really liked her now. The trouble was that the mushroom cloud was growing, and Scilla still didn't know what to say.

Scilla was rescued from her dilemma by the patter of rain-drops on the window. You'd have thought those drops were the cavalry coming to the rescue. If he'd had a flag, Beamer would have waved it wildly, cheering till his lungs wore out.

"Hey, we'd better get going before it really starts coming down," Scilla said quickly. "Thanks for having us over," she said to Alana with a smile. "I've had a great time!"

"Me too," said Beamer.

"No question about it," added Ghoulie.

Scilla hesitated a moment then hugged her. Alana's eyes grew big with surprise and bewilderment. She had no idea how to react. Then Alana moved toward Ghoulie.

Ghoulie backtracked triple speed, disguising his retreat with a laugh and a crooked smile. "See you next time. Yessiree, just put up that flag, and we'll be back here in a flash!" Then he was in the hallway, making a quick run to the balcony window.

Fearing the same thing as Ghoulie, Beamer also made a quick exit. He took her outstretched hand and shook it like he was pumping water from a well. "Yeah, let us know, and we'll be back. Some day maybe you can come and visit us—well, maybe when we find a way to change your dad's mind ... and ... and a few other things."

"Some things are just for girls," Scilla said to Alana with a wink, "like hugs."

Alana batted her eyelashes, trying to figure out what a wink was all about, but she nodded, seeming to get the gist of Scilla's comment.

"We'll see you soon. Oh, let me help a little," Scilla said as she scurried about the room, putting things back the way they were. "We don't want anyone to know you've had visitors."

"That's okay," Alana answered, "I'll clean up. You'd better get going before you get drenched in a downpour."

"Oh, yeah, right!" Scilla said. "Well, bye!"

Alana was right behind her when she ran out the door, and she was waving at them from the balcony when they disappeared into the canopy of leaves.

* * * * *

Sure enough, Scilla got grounded ... for two whole weeks! Her grandmother could hardly speak to her, except through clenched teeth. Dashiell told their grandmother that it had been an accident. Once again, Scilla was about to be grateful for her stepbrother when he added that Scilla probably shouldn't have been playing near something as fragile as that lamp. Scilla wasn't sure she appreciated him coming to her defense. His other attempts to comfort Scilla involved describing his latest science project. Scilla thought it sounded familiar, but she couldn't quite place it.

After a week of listening to Dashiell brag about his accomplishments, Scilla gave in to doing a little bragging on her own. She told him about the caves full of fireflies and about Parker's Castle and its bizarre garden, about the miniature world in the cavern, Solomon's palatial mansion that looked like a train locomotive, and about the giant web. Dashiell gave her a doubtful look with each story, but that's what eventually ended her period of grounding six days early. Dashiell got their grandma to let Scilla show him the things she'd talked about. Her grandma had always taken Scilla's stories with a raised eyebrow or two—you know, the old "overactive imagination" explanation. She said as much to Dashiell, but he insisted that he wanted to see for himself.

Scilla was looking forward to gaining a little respect. Unfortunately, things didn't turn out like she'd hoped. First of all, the fireflies hadn't awakened from their winter nap, and the caves were dark and cold and dripping with water.

At least the lamps worked, but Dashiell was unimpressed, believing that a battery-powered lightbulb was buried in that yellow-green liquid. Then Scilla couldn't find the way to the miniature world. The smirk on Dashiell's face did nothing to help her rising level of frustration. She finally got totally lost and had to call Ghoulie to rescue them by tracking her phone via GPS.

As if that wasn't enough, when they finally got back to the surface and into Ms. Parker's garden, it was all covered with plastic. She was having it fertilized and treated with bug killer. They coughed all the way to the iron gate. After she got home, Scilla sat in front of her mirror for a half hour waiting for her face to shrivel up from the toxic fumes. She was sure that her grandmother would be mad enough to bury her without even her name on the tombstone. Of course, her stepbrother's funeral would probably be on national television.

Ghoulie, who was still with Scilla after rescuing them from the cave, finally convinced her to take Dashiell the few blocks over to Solomon Parker's house. That way they could see his house and probably get him to let them into the miniature world. On the way, Dashiell talked about how he had been recruited by NASA and how he had discovered a new planet around a star that was later named after him. Ghoulie rolled his eyes.

Unfortunately, this was not Scilla's day. All they ended up seeing at Solomon Parker's estate was the wall and gate. Solomon was away on a trip to visit the architect for the new trolley station. Meanwhile, his staff of servants was doing spring cleaning.

Scilla's expression was drooping severely when they got back to her house. Naturally, things would get worse.

11
Banished!

Now that Scilla was no longer grounded, Beamer told her they were overdue in visiting Alana. The flag had come and gone three times without them visiting her. The boys had worried about hurting the girl's feelings, but not enough to go without Scilla.

Again they talked about how they had to be careful with the girl. One thing Scilla was not going to do was brag. She'd learned her lesson. She didn't know how Dashiell got away with doing it so much, but she was turning off the spigot. "Show not tell" was her new catchphrase.

* * * * *

Alana greeted them like they were long-lost relatives. "Oh, I was afraid I'd never see you again!" she cried, almost in tears. "Every chance I had, I put the flag out, but you never came!"

Clearly the girl had been close to frantic. Suddenly Beamer was sorry that he and Ghoulie hadn't come over. They could have, at least, let her know that the problem had nothing to do with her.

"I worried so much," she went on, now wiping a tear off her cheek. "Daddy would ask me what was wrong, but I couldn't tell him, of course. I felt bad about it. He gets so worried when I'm hurt or sad."

Scilla got busy telling her what had happened. She had a very difficult time describing what the word *grounded* meant. *Is it possible that the girl has never done anything wrong?* For a moment, Beamer wondered if she was one of those "little miss perfect" girls. *No*, he concluded. *The girl is just so ... innocent—that was it! She was like a puppy or a kitten—completely innocent!*

She was about as excitable as a puppy too. She would play with such energy and giggle and laugh so hard that she would almost get out of breath.

This visit, they spent most of their time in the castle playhouse. He and Ghoulie had suggested the idea when they found some play swords, shields, and helmets. Of course, they had to ignore the fact that they were pink. Beamer would yell from the highest tower how he would defend the castle to his last drop of blood, while Ghoulie would ride up to the castle calling out challenges. Yes, *ride* is what he did, and not on a stick with a horse's head. Alana had a real pony parked in a little corral at the corner of her yard. It was one of the few things around that wasn't pink.

What Beamer liked especially was the cannon. It sat on top of the castle wall and actually fired plastic cannonballs—pink ones, of course.

Alana seemed very happy to be a maiden in distress and to be rescued from imprisonment in one tower or another. She even found a Sleeping Beauty costume to wear. It was hard not to stare at the girl. Her face looked so out of place in the costume. Beamer could see the same reaction in the eyes of Scilla and Ghoulie and hoped that Alana wouldn't notice.

Naturally, Scilla would have none of this maiden-in-distress stuff. Nor would she ask politely to wield a sword. Once, when Beamer rode the pony up close to the castle, she suddenly swung out from behind the castle on a pink rope. She knocked Beamer off the pony, taking his sword and shield in the process.

Beamer was severely bummed by this and chased her and the pony all over the yard, up, around, and through the castle, while Ghoulie and Alana laughed and laughed. Beamer was hard-pressed to figure out what was so funny. That was when he learned there was such a thing as having too much fun. Alana suddenly jumped back and gave a little "eeek." There, standing on the open stone patio outside the back door, was the nanny with the pointed nose. She didn't just look upset; *volcanic* might be a good description.

"What *aah* you children doing *heah*?" she asked on the verge of eruption. "I told you that Alana could have no *visitahs*! Get out of here right now *befoah* I call the police!"

"But Nanna," Alana said, trying to defend them, "I asked them to come over."

"Out! Out!" Ms. Warrington continued to scream as she scurried down the broad course of steps into the backyard.

Scilla threw down her sword and shield as Ghoulie scrambled around the winding steps of the castle and hopped on the pony behind her. They were going to have to move quickly to get out of this yard before the fire-breathing woman caught up with them. They galloped over to Beamer, who was still out of breath from chasing Scilla. Ghoulie reached down and hoisted him up by one arm, but Beamer somehow ended up sitting backward on the pony. Luckily it was a big pony, and Scilla weighed only a little more than a feather.

As they galloped toward the tree, Beamer yelled, "We weren't trying to hurt her. We were trying to be nice." The lady's expression didn't soften. Beamer gave up, figuring they'd have better luck feeding candy to a vampire.

As they approached the tree, Alana was running toward them. "Please come back!" she pleaded with them. "I'll find a way."

They lofted onto a couple of branches and swung into the tree as the horse ran under it. Beamer thought it was a pretty cool trick. He was wondering if they might have a career doing pony tricks in a circus. But then he saw Ghoulie hanging from the tree by one leg with his glasses on sideways. Ghoulie managed to scramble up out of the way just before the woman ran beneath the tree.

"Don't you *evah* come back!" she yelled up at them. "Do you *heah* me? The next time I will call the police!"

Beamer looked back as they climbed. He saw the woman take Alana into her arms. "*Aah* you all *raht*?" he heard her ask Alana. "What did they say to you?" Their voices grew fainter as the woman walked the girl back toward the house.

They were all gasping up air like they were on Mars without a space suit. "Well, that's that." Ghoulie coughed. "We take one more step in that house, and she'll have us on a table in the morgue."

"She wasn't just angry," said Scilla thoughtfully. "Did you notice?"

"Yeah," said Beamer, "she was scared—terrified even."

"Like a lioness protecting her cub," Scilla finished for him. "Knowin' Alana's condition, I guess I can understand. Do you suppose she's her real mother?"

"Uh ... Scilla," said Ghoulie with a wry look, "we saw her mother's picture. Remember? And Pinocchio looks more like this woman than Alana does."

* * * * *

There could have been all sorts of reasons — they weren't used to climbing the tree from the ground up or they were dizzy from their quick escape or the wind had a little pixie dust in it — but they couldn't find the passage, at least for a very long time. And when they did, it didn't look right. They weren't even in the same tree. Ghoulie checked his combination compass, GPS tracker, and odor analyzer and gave them a direction. Pretty soon, though, it was clear that they were going the wrong way. They could tell they were in the same neighborhood, though; the houses were just as strange. The one they were now passing was off-the-chart strange. It had a broad, flat roof that was almost completely covered with trees!

Beamer was totally befuddled. *How could anyone plant a forest on top of a house? Where would the roots go?* The trees weren't all that big, but the canopy of leaves was pretty dense. Even with shafts of light from the setting sun prying into every nook and cranny, the forest interior looked very murky.

This was no time to explore. Night was looming in the east, and they were already late for supper. Ghoulie tried to call home, but his cell phone was dead. As it turned out, so were Beamer's and Scilla's. Good grief! They couldn't be more than a half mile from home. Before they had time to think about it, things became even more complicated.

A stream of moths suddenly poured out from the forest and crossed directly in front of them. On second glance, Beamer wasn't sure they were moths. It was really too early in the year for moths, and these were kind of big, the size of a small bird. They were almost white, but not quite. Actually, they were a lot of different colors—blue, green, pink, and yellow—all just slightly off from white. They were so bright that they seemed to glow. Come to think of it, they were doing just that—glowing.

12

The Enchanted Forest

"Hey ... y'all," said Scilla in a hushed voice. "Do you see what I see?"

"Uhhhh ... probably not, because I'm sure I'm dreaming," said Ghoulie.

"I'm not sayin'," said Beamer, "because I don't want anyone to think I'm crazy."

"Then I'll say it," said Scilla. "Those moths don't have insect bodies."

"But they're not really ... human, are they?" asked Beamer with a squeak in his voice.

"Maybe they're fairies," said Scilla with hushed excitement. "I'm gonna find out." She immediately tumbled off the branch, caught another, and swung over to drop onto the forest path.

Somebody oughtta check her DNA, thought Beamer. *There's gotta be some chimpanzee in there somewhere.* "Scilla!" whisper-shouted Beamer. "Where are you going? We don't even know if they're friendly."

It didn't look like they were going to find out, for as soon as Scilla plunked down on the roof in front of them, the moths shot back into the forest.

"Stop!" cried Scilla. "I won't hurt you! I promise!"

But it wasn't her they were afraid of. They heard flapping wings—loud and leathery. Then they heard a shriek!

Scilla whirled around and looked up. She lurched back, fell to the ground with a scream, and then lay there without moving. Beamer and Ghoulie recoiled back into a thicket of tree leaves. The thing flapping its wings and hovering far too near Scilla was right out of a nightmare. It had the wings of a bat and the face of a monster.

"It's a gargoyle!" Ghoulie exclaimed in hushed alarm. "We've got to get Scilla away from him!"

But the gargoyle paid no attention to Scilla. It flew quickly off in pursuit of the moths. Beamer and Ghoulie lost no time in getting to Scilla. Ghoulie checked her pulse, and Beamer listened to her heart.

"What are y'all doing?" she suddenly yelped as she pushed them off her. "This is no time to play paramedic. That thing is after the fairies. We've gotta rescue them!"

"Are you sure they're fairies?" Beamer asked her. "Did they say anything? What did they look like?"

"First of all, the moths weren't human," she said after taking a deep breath. "They were sort of human, but their eyes were too big and shaped like ... uh, maybe rounded diamonds. And their legs were too long and spindly, like insect legs."

"Whoa! They'd be great for a science fair exhibit!" said Ghoulie. "Could we get rights for a national tour?"

"Would y'all pipe down!" Scilla yelled in frustration as

she waved a "Back off" to them. "Come on, we gotta save them!" Scilla said, suddenly bolting on down the path into the roof forest.

"Scilla!" Beamer yelled again. "We don't have anything to fight gargoyles with! Scillllaaaaa!"

But Scilla had already charged into a dark corner of the forest. "Oh, brother!" Beamer said with a sigh. "Looks like we're gonna have to drag her back. Let's go, Ghoulie," he said, charging after her.

The forest was every bit as murky as it had looked from afar. The tree trunks were especially weird. They weren't tucked neatly into the ground like most trees on Murphy Street—or on any other street Beamer had ever been on. They stood above the ground on their partly exposed roots, looking like they might start walking at any moment. The normal assortment of forest animals was skittering around—squirrels, chipmunks, rabbits, and the like—even a deer or two. There were also a lot of fireflies beginning to whisk about as it got darker.

Something didn't seem right about all this wildlife to Beamer, though. First of all, he'd never seen so many forest creatures at the same time. Second, all the animals seemed like they'd just jumped out of *Bambi* or *Snow White*. They were just too perfect—like out of a cartoon forest. Even the weeds were pretty with flowers.

Also, unlike most forests, this forest floor was covered with grass. Real grass needed plenty of sunlight, which you couldn't get in a dense forest. What's more, the grass was neatly trimmed, not a blade out of place. Beamer was seeing all this on the run, of course. Luckily his legs were longer than Scilla's. "Scillaaaa, stop!" he yelled as he drew closer to her. "Scillaaaa!" he called again as he dived for her.

He missed her and rolled across the grass. "Hey, what is this stuff?" he asked as he ran his hands across the turf. The grass was soft and warm ... like fur! "This is too crazy!" exclaimed Beamer. Beamer picked up a fallen leaf and handed it to Scilla as she came back to see if he was all right. "When's the last time you held a soft and furry leaf?" he asked as Ghoulie caught up with them and reached to touch the leaf in her hand.

Before Scilla could say anything, they heard a moan, or was it a muffled roar? They froze in their tracks and scanned the gloomy depths of the forest.

"That didn't sound soft and fury," Ghoulie said in a hushed voice.

Very carefully, they stood up and started walking toward the sound. For some reason they seemed to be huddled close together, sort of like Dorothy and her friends in the dark forest of Oz. Ghoulie looked a strong match for the Tin Man, but Beamer wasn't keen on being either the Cowardly Lion or the Scarecrow. The forest path took a sharp turn to the left. It was when they rounded that turn that their stomachs fell.

Directly ahead, stretched out between two trees, was a huge spiderweb almost as big as the one in Beamer's attic! The gargoyle was flapping about in front of the web, stalking the fairies who were fearfully scattering in a circle away from it. Beamer saw that one of the fairies was caught in the web. He thought maybe the other fairies were trying to keep the gargoyle away from their friend. Then the danger level jumped to critical. The spindly legs of an enormous spider suddenly appeared through the trees heading into the web. The gargoyle jumped back with a loud shriek!

"No way can we handle both a gargoyle and a giant spider,"

said Beamer. They didn't wait to see whether the spider or the gargoyle would win the day. They shifted into full reverse, then spun about and ran full tilt back the way they had come.

Before they got ten steps, though, somebody turned off the forest!

Suddenly they were on an empty flat roof. The weird trees, cute animals, flowers, and birds were all gone! So were the fairies, they noticed when they turned around. But two trees still stood in a small garden plot on one side of the roof. And the web was still there too, with the spider making its way down the web toward the roof floor.

Whoa! Eight legs against six isn't fair! "Move it, guys!" Beamer yelled. "Molgotha's gonna be on our tail any second!" There wasn't time to figure out what was going on. All they had time to think about was moving their legs.

They ran till their tongues were hanging out and their legs were turning to rubber. They didn't even stop to climb, but launched into a web of tree foliage. Then they scrambled through the branches like tree nymphs, stumbling from tree to tree, going they knew not where. Twenty minutes later, they finally felt safe enough to stop and catch their breaths. They sat quietly, listening for anything that sounded like what might be a giant spider pushing through the leaves.

By now it was pretty dark but, thanks to an ancient streetlight, they recognized the street corner below them. It was the corner of Murphy Street and Parkview, the street that ran directly into the park. With no tree passage in sight, they found a cluster of both large and small trees and climbed down to the street. Unfortunately, they all got home just in time to be grounded for getting home late.

* * * * *

Beamer didn't sleep very well that night. Molgotha was alive! At least he thought it was Molgotha. *After all, how many giant spiders could there be in one neighborhood?* The MacIntyre Web had the uncanny ability to absorb and radiate energy—not exactly a practical function for a spiderweb. The web in the enchanted forest seemed to function more like a normal web—too bad for that trapped fairy.

Everything had happened so fast! And what was that disappearing act all about? Oh well, what was one more mystery to the Star-Fighters? The trouble with the forest was that they'd been lost when they found it and still lost when they escaped it. Beamer didn't have a clue how to find it again.

13

Monster Bash

Any way you find them, spiders and spiderwebs tend to make people squirm. Dashiell nearly fell backward down the stairs when he saw the MacIntyre Web. He wasn't supposed to be on the attic steps, of course. Nobody was, except for the scientists.

Once Scilla was through being grounded again—just for a day this time — Dashiell had insisted on following her around. Scilla clearly wasn't excited about the idea. She'd told Ghoulie how Dashiell had gotten a lot of mileage making fun of Scilla's "imagined" adventures after their disappointing tour.

Ghoulie was pretty sure that Dashiell wasn't all he was cracked up to be. Scilla had told him about Dashiell's science project. Ghoulie had won first prize when he'd done that project two years ago. He'd even put it up online. He showed the site to Beamer. They hadn't said anything to Scilla, though. After all, he was her brother, and, for some reason, she idolized him.

Anyway, the kids had all been gathered in Beamer's room when Dashiell just slipped away. Beamer was showing them the new section he had added to his wall-length Lego monorail system.

Dashiell, however, was more interested in proving, once and for all, that his stepsister was a loony tune. Seeing the real McCoy web was a real blow to Dashiell. Before he could stop himself, he yelped.

The next thing he knew he was surrounded by scientists angry at him for intruding.

"Dashiell, what are you doing?" Scilla called as she clambered up the stairs. "We're not supposed to go up here!"

Oh, great, here comes the rest of the funny farm, Dashiell thought as he saw Beamer and Ghoulie right behind his sister. He quickly recovered from his momentary lapse of cool, though. To tell the truth, Dashiell was pretty impressed with the web and the scientific equipment around it. He had a hard time restraining the urge to punch, twist, and turn every control device he saw. But he had no intention of letting on. He'd spent a lot of time promoting himself as the authority on just about everything. So he had to let them know he was on top of things. The scientists seemed frozen in shock as he swaggered across the attic. He spouted out a few facts about spiders, things he'd heard in somebody's book report. *That should be enough for these second-rate intellects*, he thought.

You see, Dashiell believed he needed to put this web business in its place. Right now, this was Scilla's thing; he had to make it his. Still acting the professor, he picked up a discarded towel rod to act as a pointer. "Notice the circular shape of the web," Dashiell said. "This is typical of the orb web spider. The female's web is smaller."

He heard a scientist choke back a laugh. *Was he getting his facts backward? Maybe the female's web is larger.* Dashiell didn't like feeling insecure. He wasn't used to it. Still, he went on: "But as big as this web is, spider silk is a very ... uh ... weak material—" He took a swipe at the web to demonstrate his point. He was surprised when it didn't break—not even close.

Suddenly he felt body blows high and low as Beamer and Ghoulie tackled him. Then he felt someone pick him up by his belt buckle. The next thing he knew, he was back in the hallway downstairs and hearing the door to the attic slam behind him.

Dashiell's face was as bright as a sunset, but Ghoulie was pretty sure he saw a thundercloud hovering above his head. At any rate, he stormed out of the house with the force of a gale wind.

"You just wait until I tell my grandma!" he yelled at the three behind him. Then he pointed at his stepsister, screaming, "You think you've been in trouble before, just wait! Letting the bird out of the cage was nothing! Rigging the trip wire to make the lamp fall over when you passed by was something else. I can do that kind of stuff all day, and Grandma will never know. You're going to look like a walking catastrophe before I'm through with you!"

That's when an acorn bopped him on the head. He looked up. His grandmother was leaning out her second-floor window, staring at him through a major scowl.

"Dashiell, you and I need to have a little talk," she said before she pulled back through the window and slammed it closed.

Dashiell's voice dropped to a hush, but it was a voice

filled with venom. "I'll get you!" he growled through clenched teeth. "I'll get you all."

He then spun around and stalked toward the tree. "I know about your stupid tree house and the Star-Fighters," he said with a mocking laugh. "Star-Fighters!" he spat. "Who do you think you're kidding?"

Dashiell burst out laughing even harder when he saw the plywood, pulley-driven elevator. "I could have done better with rubber bands and Popsicle sticks," he said. "And you call this a transporter?"

When Dashiell reached a point about halfway up the tree, Ghoulie expected the tree to react to Dashiell's bad intentions. When that didn't happen, Ghoulie asked Beamer, "What's wrong with the tree? It should have bumped him out by now—you know, the hurricane winds, the plague of insects and all?"

"I don't know," said Beamer. "Maybe the tree is worried about Scilla's feelings or—"

"No," insisted Ghoulie, "all that the field around the tree does is sense the brain-wave pattern."

"He's definitely not nice," Beamer said with a grimace, "but maybe it's because he has no intention of physically hurting anybody or anything."

"Sticks and stones, huh?" muttered Ghoulie.

"I guess," said Beamer with a shrug. "I never did like that saying, though. It always seemed to me that cuts and scratches healed a lot faster than hurts from words."

As the transporter drew closer to the tree ship, Dashiell had even more things to say: "Talk about a rat trap!" he said with another twisted laugh. "That ship is nothing but splinters in the making. Are you sure it's not going to blow down with the next breeze?"

Ghoulie was really getting tired of hearing Dashiell's laugh. At that moment the wind picked up and he felt his hopes reviving.

But then the transporter bumped into its dock near the ship. "Hey, Scilla!" Dashiell shouted down to her. "Where did you say you've been in this termite nest? You have a better chance of finding aliens on a skateboard!"

Then the door to the tree ship opened, and someone stepped out. Dashiell screamed, and they both disappeared!

For a moment, nobody said anything.

"What . . . what happened?" Scilla finally asked.

"Where did they go?" Ghoulie asked at almost the same time.

Two heartbeats later, all three of them were scrambling up the tree.

"Somebody was up there with him," Scilla gasped. "Somebody who came out of the ship."

"Did anybody see who it was?" Beamer asked.

"I just heard the door open," Ghoulie said. "Then there was the scream."

"Who could it be? Jared? Jack?"

"Don't know," said Beamer as he pulled himself up on the ramp. "But we gotta find both of them faster than light!"

14

Rock and Roll

Dashiell had no idea where he was, except that it was dark. Wherever he was, the sound of his scream still echoed around like he was in an underground cavern. *What did I see? It was a monster—that was for sure. Where is it now?* He backed away from what he could not see. Then he began to sense a faint light. His eyes were adjusting. Slowly coming into view before him was the same creature he'd seen in the tree. He screamed again!

"What are you screaming about?" the creature asked, pumping her arms and fists down to her side in irritation. "Could you please quiet down before you break my eardrums?"

It's a girl, thought Dashiell in amazement, the ugliest girl I've ever seen. "I ... I ... What ... Where ...?" he gasped. "You ... you're — " he started. But then a whole sea of yellow eyes emerged from rocks and crevices behind the girl. Their eyes seemed to glow in the dark.

Dashiell backed away as these new creatures approached.

The ugly girl, who didn't see them behind her, looked puzzled at his reaction. Then, when they were close enough that she probably felt their hot breath on her neck, she finally whipped around. She gave a shrill squeal and bolted back into Dashiell, who jumped immediately back from her.

The faces of the creatures with the glowing eyes became more visible. Their skin, which was very wrinkled and pale, glowed a light, phosphorescent green. But what puzzled Dashiell the most was how they crowded around the ugly girl. They shied away from him like he was a leper. But they were all over her, fondling her blonde hair and her clothing. If they kept this up, she had a good chance of being both bald and dressed in shreds very soon. In fact, they seemed to be fawning over her like she was a beauty queen or a goddess.

*   *   *   *   *

Ghoulie had concluded that Dashiell and his unwilling companion had been sent somewhere by the ship's transporter, which was suddenly acting like a real transporter. They had no idea how to find out where they had gone, though, not as long as the ship remained in the tree.

But something was happening. Beamer was already wearing his uniform, and the tree ship was slowly morphing into something other than plywood.

"It couldn't have sent them too far," said Ghoulie as he ran to his crayon-painted instrument panel. "Come on, ship, take off!" he muttered, banging the plywood panel. "Take off!" The trouble, of course, was that, until the ship "took off," those instruments would stay just paint on plywood.

There was nothing to read. But even as he stared at it, the panel began to transform into the razzle-dazzle display familiar in their adventures.

"It's happening," said Beamer, who was already looking more mature in his uniform, "just much slower than usual."

"We need to get out of this tree now!" yelled Scilla, becoming more distressed by the second.

"Hit the thruster switches, Ghoulie, and see what happens," Beamer said.

Nothing happened. "Okay, okay," Ghoulie said as he took some deep breaths. "Let's all calm down. It's just not ready yet."

They all breathed deeply and either sat down or leaned against something. Scilla, whose jeans were turning into an ensign's uniform, looked up at Beamer. "Didn't you once say that when the meteor struck this tree, it was like . . . uh . . . 'the finger of God touched the earth'?"

"That was Old Lady—I mean Ms.—Parker who said it," Beamer answered. "But you're right. God's in charge even if his timing sometimes seems a little slow."

The next thing Scilla heard was a lot of bleeping and clicking and whirring. She turned and saw that her instrument panel was all lit up. Then she wasn't Scilla anymore.

Ensign Bruzelski quickly flicked through a number of screens on her monitor. That's when she noticed a holographic image visible in the middle of the room. She had the strangest feeling that she hadn't seen this holographic 3-D star chart before. But the thought faded, and she continued as if it had always been available. One point in the chart was highlighted. She zoomed in and said, "Hey, y'all, like I thought, they've been transported away, all right, but not too far away — well, within the solar system, anyway."

"Then get us there!" Captain MacIntyre ordered. "Ignition!"

Suddenly they were traveling through what seemed to be a many-colored fog bank. They felt heavy, like their feet and legs were chained to concrete — their skin stretched like it was made of rubber.

"Ives!" the captain said. "Where have you put us?"

Something that looked like a huge jellyfish splattered onto a window. "I'm not sure, Captain," Commander Ives said. "Looks like we're in the middle of another ocean."

"Then why do I feel like I'm wearing lead underwear and my stomach is in my big toe?" asked Ensign Bruzelski.

"Big sea ... big planet," groaned the commander with the enormous gravity stretching his lips across his face like splattered bubble gum.

Their ship gave in to the massive gravity and started to fall deeper into the multicolored sea. They fell faster and faster until it seemed as if they were dropping in an elevator. They and everything loose on the bridge hit the ceiling with a splat! Stomachs don't really like all this confusion about up and down, so they rebelled.

I knew I should have skipped the anchovies, thought Scilla as she turned green.

"Come on, baby," Commander Ives belched as he fired all thrusters, the antigravity array, as well as the electro-trashmatic, goonjammer defense array. The ship gradually slowed its fall and began to struggle back up. Everything — people and yecch — fell to the floor in a major splash.

Stars began to fade into view as the ship surged out of the soupy atmosphere.

At the same time, three huge boulders struck one another and blew apart. A spray of tiny rocks spattered across the hull like a hailstorm. Pretty soon, though, Bruzelski noticed that they were in a whole field of tiny rocks that kept splattering against the hull. Some of them stuck like chewing gum and began to build up into globs.

"Take us somewhere else!" the captain commanded as he and Bruzelski stuffed chewing gum into the tiny airholes created by the stones.

Commander Ives hit the aft thrusters. They burst out of the hailstorm — not exactly into empty space, but to where you could see the rocks coming at least one at a time.

"Give us a view aft," ordered Captain MacIntyre.

Aft ... aft ... aft ... Scilla couldn't remember what *aft* meant. Her ensign self knew, of course, but, in all the excitement, she'd sort of lost ... herself.

"Get a move on, Ensign," the captain growled.

Aft ... What's aft?

"I'm on it, Captain — just a little technical difficulty," the ensign said, feeling more like Scilla than Ensign Bruzelski.

Scilla had never heard Beamer growl before. But then the captain wasn't exactly Beamer, was he? She didn't think they'd taught her the word *aft* in her first six grades. That left TV and movies — oh yeah, *aft*, that's the rear, yes, rear view.

"Got it, Captain," the ensign who was Scilla said.

Their view screen wasn't *Star Trek* size, but it was still twice as big as most home-theater gizmos. So, when the lower-left corner of a huge yellow planet filled the top-right half of the screen, it was a sight that took their breaths away. Circling around the planet was a massive set of rock-strewn rings that cut diagonally all the way across the screen.

"It's Saturn," the ensign said in hushed reverence.

Yeah, Scilla knew all about Saturn. Ten times the size of Earth, it was the second largest planet in the solar system. Let's see, last I heard it had over sixty moons —

Blee, blee, blee! An alarm sounded!

"Watch where you're going!" the captain shouted at the same time.

The view screen switched to the front. Straight ahead, filling most of the screen, was a cloud-shrouded moon.

"Land — uh, moon dead ahead!" cried the ensign.

"Not the best choice of words," the commander said as his hands flew over the instruments. "Whew, sure is crowded around here!"

"Get her nose up," the captain yelled as they dived into the murky atmosphere.

They jostled around a bit, and finally the clouds began to clear.

"This doesn't fit at all!" said the captain. The surface looked earth-like. "Zoom in!" he ordered.

"Aye, Captain," answered the ensign. The picture adjusted and they could see that the surface was covered with forests, lakes, grasslands, and waterfalls. "We're a long way from the sun. It should be as cold as ice down there. Which moon did you say this was?"

"Didn't have time to figure it out," said the commander, "but I think the thick layer of clouds must have caused a greenhouse effect that heated up this moon."

"It would be pretty if it weren't for the pimples," said the ensign.

"What do you mean, pimples?" asked the captain.

"I saw them too," said the commander. "Gray-colored bumps scattered a hundred miles or so apart across the surface."

"And we're going to crash into one of them if you don't pull up," the ensign shouted at the commander.

Commander Ives pulled the ship up at the last second, enough for them to skid across the surface like a rocket-powered sled. Slowing down the ship, though, was another thing.

"Uh ... Commander," the ensign said with a gulp. One of those pimples was growing pretty big in their view screen.

The commander punched the reverse thrusters. Gradually their skid slowed. It looked like he might pull it off. But then Bruzelski felt a slight bump. That was apparently enough to trigger something. The pimple didn't pop but it began to open, layer after layer, like an onion being peeled.

"What in blazes have we bumped into?" asked the commander in a hushed voice.

15

Mole People

Inside the pimple, or bubble, was something that looked like a honeycomb ... actually more like a mountain of honeycombs. The honeycombs were connected by steps and walkways and bridges that crossed streams or rock gorges or streets.

After testing the atmosphere, the captain and Ensign Bruzelski emerged from a set of steps that folded down from beneath the ship.

A faint part of the captain that was still Beamer remembered that they didn't have a door like this on the tree ship.

The captain didn't see any trees or plants in the bubble city, except for what looked like several varieties of fluorescent moss and some mushrooms big enough to be small trees.

"The city must be a mile across," said Bruzelski as she

surveyed the honeycomb structures, which spread through the giant
circle into the distance. "But where are all the people?"

Hardly anything was moving except the wind. Then they heard
tiny voices.

The ensign shielded her eyes from the bright circle in the sky
behind which the ringed planet hovered, and she peered across the
honeycomb landscape. "Captain, over there," she said, pointing
toward the right. "Two figures appear to be running this way."

Captain MacIntyre took a device out of his pocket, which he
put on like a headband. A small screen flipped out from the band
and expanded in front of his eyes. Now he could see clearly two
people running, waving, and yelling at them.

Beamer thought the device was pretty cool, but it was apparently old news to the captain.

"Well, Bruzelski," he said calmly, "it looks like we've found your
stepbrother. The other one appears to be a civilian woman."

Beamer was startled. The captain knew about Dashiell! It
was funny, though, he didn't seem to know him personally
like Beamer did.

"Scilla ... Beamer!" Alana cried happily when she was close
enough to recognize them. Then she twisted around and called
back, with her hands circling her mouth. "It's all right! You can
come out! They won't hurt you!"

At least that's what she meant to be saying. What the captain
heard coming from her mouth was a flood of clicks and other
sounds you might mistake as someone gargling in the bathroom.

Cringing and shielding themselves from the outdoor light,

creatures began to stir out of their hiding places. With their big yellow eyes, very pale, wrinkled skin, and long, white hair, they gave a whole new meaning to the word ugly. Of course, they probably had a similar impression of the Star-Fighters.

As word spread on back through the city, crowds of them — hundreds and then thousands — soon appeared. Like little two-legged blobs of wrinkles, they moved up steps and walkways toward the edge of their flattened dome to look out in wonder over the landscape.

The captain tapped his communicator. "What do you have, Ives?" he asked. "What's going on here?"

He immediately heard the commander's voice. "Captain, I've been running their electronic transmissions through the universal translator. They seem to be thanking some golden goddess for saving them."

The captain turned off his communicator as Dashiell and the girl he now vaguely recognized as Ms. Franck approached the ship. Their clothing looked strange — just colorless cloth wrapped around them, mummy-like, from their shoulders to their knees.

Almost out of breath from her long run, Ms. Franck stopped abruptly, giving them a puzzled look. "You are Beamer and Scilla, aren't you? You look like them but older or something."

The captain shook his head thoughtfully. The name Beamer did sound familiar, though he wasn't sure why. "Not exactly, but I think we can take you to them."

"What took you so long?" Dashiell asked. "We've been here for weeks!"

"Weeks?" exclaimed Ensign Bruzelski. "But we just left — "
Suddenly she wasn't sure where they had left and when. After all,
Star-Fighter patrols could last months at a time. Like the captain,
her connection to her earthly counterpart was very faint. Scilla
and her memories were like shadows in the ensign's mind.

"These creatures haven't been on the surface of their world for
eons!" Ms. Franck said excitedly.

"It took us a while to learn their language," said Dashiell.
"Actually, they wouldn't talk much to me," he said almost timidly.
"Would you believe, they were grossed out by the sight of me?" He
gave an embarrassed laugh and went on. "Not by her, though. She
was Beauty and I was the Beast."

"Yes, and I don't understand why," the girl said sheepishly. "I
think he's very handsome."

"Anyway, what's their story?" the captain asked, taking out his
recorder.

"Well, one day very long ago, their world was pelted with
rocks from the sky," Ms Franck explained. "More and more came
each day, bombarding their houses and streets."

"Their moon must have veered into the orbit of Saturn's rings,"
the captain said, looking up toward the brightest part of the
cloudy sky.

"A moon? This is a moon?" Dashiell asked in amazement. "Wow!
Well, anyway, they moved underground to avoid the bombardment.
Then they covered their settlement with large, unbreakable metal
shells and just stayed there."

Mole People

Commander Ives's voice erupted from the captain's communicator. "Hey, Captain," he said. "Inhabitants from this settlement are trying to persuade the inhabitants of the other shells to open up. Talk about a major squabble! The universal translator isn't picking up everything, but it sounds like most of the others are afraid. In fact, I just heard one transmission in which another settlement accused this one of trying to deceive them. Here, let me patch you in."

"Don't you understand?" the captain heard a deep, rumbling voice ask above the other screeching voices online. "The bombardment stopped centuries ago. The danger is gone!" More voices rose in protest, but the first voice shouted above the others, "Take heed, I'm seeing green hills, rivers, and waterfalls. We've let our fears keep us from enjoying the beauty and bounty of our world long enough."

The radio argument continued on the rest of the day. From what the captain could gather from Ms. Franck's translations, it looked like it might take another eon before all the cities would trust their world enough to open up. That night, the local "mole people," as the captain called them, held a big celebration in the center of the city. There was much more to the city than the captain had at first thought. Most of the city — about three times as much as they had seen on the surface — was belowground.

Thanks to the big planet glowing beyond the cloud layer, night here was not that dark. Of course, the thick cloud layer had kept the mole people from knowing about the planet above them, or the stars either, for that matter. In fact, when the Star-Fighters tried to tell them about the beautiful ringed planet, most of the excessively wrinkled population just laughed, believing that the story was a silly fairy tale.

The next morning, tears rolled down her wrinkled cheeks and over her rumpled chin as Ms. Franck said good-bye to all the friends she had made among the mole people. The fact that the people believed the girl to be a goddess troubled the captain. Ms. Franck tried to discourage such ideas, but many of the mole people clung to them anyway.

Several minutes later the ship took off and plunged into the moon's cloud layer.

* * * * *

It was raining when the ship came out of the clouds. Beamer flinched at a lightning flash and noticed that they were back in the tree. Alana was next to him, her eyes wide in wonder.

He watched her as she walked about the tree ship and touched the plywood fixtures. She looked at her watch and shook her head in wonder. "I went to this strange place far away and stayed there for weeks," she said in a voice that seemed almost ready to break into joy, "and yet I just climbed into the tree only a few minutes ago. Is that possible?"

"Alana, how did you get here?" he asked. "We never saw you come over."

"Oh, I … I came through the trees, like you described to me. After you left last time, I explained to Ms. Warrington and Daddy how nice you all had been to me and how you were not evil at all. Daddy was so happy that I had friends to play with. He wants to meet you, though. Isn't it wonderful?"

Beamer had never seen Alana so happy. She was wide-eyed with excitement, her eyes shining bright within that crinkled face. Her alien clothing had dissolved into twenty-first-century

American attire. From the looks of her pink dress, she'd not thought what could happen to a dress when you climbed through trees. Her nanny was not going to be happy.

"What happened to that big, fancy ship you picked us up in?" she asked.

"Uhhhhh ... this is it," he said.

"But, but, but, but how did we get there ... and how did you get there ... and how did we get back here ... and ... and how ...?" Dashiell asked in a flurry of words.

"Uh ... all good questions," Ghoulie answered, "for which we have few answers. All we know is that, for some reason, the ship's transporter beamed you to a moon of Saturn."

"It's not even supposed to work," Scilla jumped in, "until the tree ship transforms from this plywood box you see now to the fancy one that picked you up."

"But that's amazing!" exclaimed Dashiell. "How do you do it?"

"Uh, we don't," Beamer answered. "We don't know why or how the ship transforms. We don't even know when it'll happen."

"As you noticed," Ghoulie said, taking another turn, "we get changed too and are able to do things kids couldn't normally do. It's great! It's incredible! But we can't make it happen."

"D'you mean we can't go back?" asked Alana.

"Maybe," Beamer piped in. "We've visited some places a second time, but it's never been our choice. All we know for sure is that God's in the middle of it. The story's almost a legend now," Beamer said as he went outside and leaned against the trunk. "Long ago a meteor struck this tree." He turned back to the others. "But it was the finger of God, and it made Murphy Street into a place where God works mysteriously in the lives of kids."

"Aw, man ... I could say I don't believe you," groaned Dashiell, "but I have to. I've lived through it. I've seen things ... felt things ... I'm definitely not as smart as I thought I was."

For a moment Beamer wondered if Dashiell had slipped a neuron. He actually sounded nice! Since talk was cheaper than actually being nice, he looked him straight in the eye. *Hmmm, he's either a great actor or he's had a serious brain-remodeling job.*

"I don't think I'll ever be afraid again," Alana said, almost dancing in place with excitement. "You were right," she said. "You can't let the scary things keep you from enjoying the good and beautiful things."

"I'm sorry I've been giving you such a hard time," Dashiell said to his sister. "I've always felt I had to be such a hotshot. You don't know how hard I tried to impress those people on the planet—or moon, I guess it was. I finally gave up trying to show off and found that they liked me much better when I was just a regular guy."

"He was pretty hard to live with until he did that," Alana said with a light laugh.

"Yeah," chimed in Dashiell. "No matter what I did or said, those ugly dudes on that moon avoided me like I was as ugly as sin. And you," he said with a laugh to Alana, "who look just like them—except for the hair, of course—they thought you were beautiful."

It happened too fast for Beamer to stop it. Alana stood there for a moment like a statue made of glass. Then her eye caught her reflection in the porthole window—the only window in the whole ship that had glass.

Alana slowly approached the window, her hands touching

her face. They could see the horror building in her expression. Suddenly she screamed! She turned and ran through them like she couldn't see them. Before they could stop her, she was out the door. They ran after her only to see her thrash through the branches and fall all the way down into the security net.

Almost out of her mind, crying more than screaming now, she scrambled out of the net and ran through the rain into the street, her arms flailing helplessly about.

The Star-Fighters stood still as the rain splattered on their hair, washed down their faces, and soaked into their T-shirts and jeans. All that time they had tried to shield her, and then, right when she seemed like the happiest girl in the world, they had shattered her like a glass figurine.

Dashiell, who had just realized what he had done, was frozen in shock. For the first time in his life, he had actually begun to care about someone other than himself. He didn't mean to hurt her. In those weeks with the mole people, he had actually come to like her. He didn't even think of her as ugly anymore. It just didn't occur to him that Alana had never seen herself in a mirror or in a windowpane or in a clear pool of water. He wasn't sure he liked caring about other people. It hurt. It really hurt!

16

The Secret in the Attic

A whole week passed without any sign of Alana. Ghoulie tried calling; Scilla tried leaving notes in the mailbox; Beamer even asked Mrs. Hotchkiss if he could deliver more study guides for Alana.

Mrs. Hotchkiss shook her head and asked, "What did you do to that family?" When Beamer seemed lost in hems and haws, she went on, "Ms. Warrington called me again and asked that, in the future, I either personally deliver the materials or send them via a courier service."

Once again Beamer's chest ached. He almost wished they hadn't tried to help the girl in the first place. *Having things go wrong is one thing, but having them go wrong when you are trying so hard to do the right thing is much harder.*

In the meantime, Scilla did something radically strange: she started doing homework. The last day before spring vacation, one of Scilla's teachers gave a pop quiz and asked for the class's homework. At the end of the day when Scilla was happily racing toward the school door, that same teacher, Mrs. Shepherd, caught her in the hallway and took her back to her classroom.

What now? Scilla asked herself as she rolled her eyes. It's not that she hadn't been in trouble before, but this shouldn't be one of those times, unless Mrs. Shepherd was mad at her for running down the hallway.

As Scilla stood in front of her desk, Mrs. Shepherd pulled out Scilla's quiz paper and her homework. She laid them side by side facing Scilla.

Scilla stared at the twin scores—100 percent. Then she looked up to see the quizzical look on Mrs. Shepherd's face. Was she accusing her of cheating?

But all she said was, "It's about time!"

Scilla was beginning to understand something. She'd been afraid. It wasn't easy to admit that. Scilla had done everything to prove how tough and independent she was. She could out-wrestle every boy her size, and she had convinced herself she didn't care if those silly, frilly girls looked down on her. No, she didn't need anybody's approval.

At least, that's what she had convinced herself. It was a lie, though. She was every bit as afraid as Alana and those mole creatures had been, except that, instead of being afraid of the unknown, she'd been afraid of failing. Everyone had told her she was smart, but what if she wasn't? What if she tried and failed? Without realizing it, she had believed that if she didn't try, it wouldn't hurt so much if she failed to match up to her brother.

She'd finally figured out that all she was doing was booby-trapping herself. There were so many things out there she could know and do. Now, at least, she was going to give it her best.

*   *   *   *   *

Some days you remember better than others. For Beamer, Easter Sunday was definitely one of them. It's not that he was this superspiritual guy. To be honest, he usually spent a lot of the time during Easter service looking forward to the famous MacIntyre Easter egg hunt. That's what his family always did after they got home from church on Easter.

This Easter morning was different, though. He got caught up more than usual in all the talking and singing about Jesus coming back to life. *Jesus made it so that death is not the end of life.* That's why there was always a lot of music and singing on Easter Sunday—the really loud and exited kind. *It's a huge celebration!*

Beamer was just beginning to figure out that there was a lot more to life than just sucking in air. Judging from what he saw on TV, some people didn't enjoy living that much. *Come to think of it, I wasn't enjoying life all that much last fall when I was trapped in that toilet stall with Jared and friends circling outside like vultures.* But for some people it was worse. They'd gotten in trouble, or their parents didn't take good care of them, or things just went wrong, like they did for Solomon Parker, who was locked inside his mansion for years. Then there was Alana, who'd been buried in that pink house for who knew how long. She looked so happy that day in the tree ship; it was like she'd come to life. Then she lost it, just like that! He couldn't help feeling it was his fault.

The MacIntyre Easter egg hunt turned out to be a blast. Ghoulie and Scilla were there. So was Dashiell, who was still being nice. They couldn't believe how many weird places an egg could be hidden. Beamer's sister, Erin, as usual, seemed to have some kind of radar for finding the chocolate ones. Yep, candy eggs were included, although Beamer had made a special request for his mom and dad, otherwise known as Mr. and Mrs. Easter Bunny, to exclude pink ones. Ghoulie used logic to figure out where eggs were hidden. Scilla, the resident tree sprite, had the upper hand in the branches.

Strangely enough, there turned out to be a lot of eggs in the tree. *Who knew that the Easter Bunny could climb trees?* Beamer cracked to himself. Scilla and Ghoulie found the fanciest egg up near the tree ship. The trouble was they found it at the same time. They bobbled it back and forth until it fell down the tree. Several other hands touched it on the way down as everybody leaped, dived, or swung through the tree for it. Both Beamer and Erin slowed it down. Dashiell tipped it into a gentle loop through the air to land in Michael's basket. The little squid head didn't even see it happen. The rest of them, though, looked at one another and shook their heads.

*　*　*　*　*

Finally, pink flag or not, the Star-Fighters decided that they had to see Alana. They sat in the tree outside her window and waited. An hour passed without their seeing so much as her shadow. They tried the balcony window, but it was now firmly locked. Then Ghoulie noticed that the attic window was cracked slightly open.

Unlike Beamer's house, Alana's Pink Palace had a flat roof. The walls of the attic were only slightly slanted inward—too steep to climb up to the attic window like you could at Beamer's place. But there was a little ledge where the third story met the attic. They climbed up the tree to where they could hop onto the ledge. Scooting along that narrow ledge, Beamer wondered if his parent's medical plan included tight-rope walking.

Getting up to the window from the ledge wasn't all that easy either. Ghoulie and Scilla had to climb up over Beamer. Beamer wished he'd made his will—you know, the written statement that tells who gets which of your belongings after you "pass on." The idea of his little brother getting his Lego monorail system made his skin crawl. Of course, his skin was already crawling every time the wind picked up and he wobbled on the ledge. At least if he survived, he'd have a career as a human ladder. Finally, Ghoulie leaned out the window and, with Scilla holding on to his legs, stretched down to pull Beamer up.

The good news was there was no giant spiderweb in this attic. The bad news took a little longer coming. The attic looked like a large medical laboratory. There were racks of chemicals and test tubes, banks of high-tech electronic equipment, and half a dozen monitor screens.

"I thought Alana's father made bug killer," Beamer said with his forehead all wrinkled.

"That's what it said on the Internet," Ghoulie said with a shrug.

"So why does he need all this hospital equipment?" Beamer asked. Sure enough, there were walls of curtains that moved on rollers, tree-like things for hanging IV bottles and bags, surgical robes and gloves, a couple of hospital beds, and some very scary-looking tools.

That's when they got the bad news. They pulled one of those rolling curtains open and nearly jumped out of their skin. There, lying on an operating table like a wrinkled Sleeping Beauty just a couple breaths this side of death, was Alana.

"What's wrong with her?" Scilla asked in a panic. "If she's sick, why isn't she in a real hospital?"

"I don't know," Beamer said as he looked around.

"Are y'all thinking what I'm thinking?" Scilla asked, her eyes supersized. "What if her dad is not her dad at all but a mad scientist! I mean, maybe he's some kind of Dr. Frankenstein who's been doing weird experiments on her."

"Come on, Scilla," grumbled Beamer as he rolled his eyes. "That's crazy."

"Yeah," she shot back at him. "But that would explain how she got ... uh, the way she is, wouldn't it?" she added, throwing the sleeping girl an uncomfortable look.

"Scilla, he's her father," Beamer said, trying to calm her down. "He's not gonna dice up his daughter."

"Are you sure about that?" she argued. "Come on, y'all; we've gotta get her outta here! Alana! Wake up, Alana!" she said, shaking the girl.

"Hey, Scilla," Ghoulie said, pulling her away from Alana. "She's all wired up with sensors and an IV. We could accidentally do something homicidal if we're not careful." He turned back to face a bank of screens. "I think these monitors are showing her vital statistics."

"Hey, guys!" Beamer whispered loudly. "I found something." He was thumbing through the pages of a notebook when the others joined him.

"It looks like some kind of research log," Ghoulie said as he leaned over Beamer's shoulder.

"There's a date for each time he wrote something down," Beamer said.

"Looks like he spilled something on the book about half-way through," said Scilla.

Looking at the book edge, Beamer could see where the pages started getting wrinkled. He leafed through to the place where the wrinkling started. "You're right. It's all very neat and organized up to here. Whoa, the ink even gets smeared a lot from here on."

"So what's that gotta do with anything?" Scilla asked, getting impatient. "We've gotta do something to get Alana out of here! He's drugged her or something."

"Look at the date!" Beamer said, his finger planted under it. "Four years and two months ago."

"There's a lot of formulas and stuff here," Ghoulie said as he took over the book and thumbed through it. "Pages and pages of them," he said, now flipping faster through the pages.

"Hey, what's that?" Beamer said, shoving his hand into the page to keep Ghoulie from turning any more. " 'Alana's aging process is beginning to accelerate.' " Beamer twisted around to read. " 'She is moving toward old age like a time machine.' "

"See! I told you," Scilla exclaimed. "He's treating her like a lab rat, injecting her with stuff to make her get older faster."

"What would be the point in that?" Beamer asked with a smirk. "Nobody wants to get old faster." Beamer turned through several more pages of technical scrawls then stopped to read, " 'So far, nothing I have given her has worked. If I don't get results soon, she will stay locked in a growth pattern that will plunge her into a painful, early death.' See, he's trying to stop her from aging so fast."

"She's dying?" Scilla asked in a choked voice.

Beamer turned a couple more pages. " 'I can't stand the thought of her suffering,' " he read again. " 'I'm the one who caused this calamity; I'm the one who must save her from it.' "

"How do you suppose he caused it?" Scilla asked worriedly.

" 'Each day I spent in tears, unable to sleep, hoping for a miracle,' " Beamer continued to read. He turned a few more pages and stopped. "Look, this one is from only a week ago: 'When she came home traumatized by the cruelty the neighborhood children had inflicted upon her—' "

"He's talking about us!" Scilla interrupted him.

" 'I knew that I had to take a chance on one more treatment.' " Beamer kept on reading.

"What kinda chance?" Scilla asked, getting more and more agitated. In frustration, she took the book from Beamer and turned to the last page with writing on it. " 'I put her to sleep,' " she read, " 'but I just couldn't bring myself to do it. One more treatment may be too much for her little body to stand.' " Scilla finished reading. "He's gonna kill her!"

17

Bug Juice

"Come on, we've gotta go for help!" Scilla said as she pushed Beamer and Ghoulie toward the window. But Ghoulie slipped away for a closer view of the bank of monitors. He had seen enough cop shows with lab technicians glued to microscopes to recognize body cells. "I bet that's Alana's bloodstream up there in lights."

"Ghoulie!" Beamer whispered a yell back at him as Scilla handed him the book and stepped through the window. "Let's get going!"

"That's funny," Ghoulie mumbled after a moment's hesitation. "The date on the screen is nearly two months ago." He punched a button and his face screwed up even more in puzzlement. But before he had time to think things through, Beamer dragged him to the window.

"Come on," Beamer said as he pushed him through the window. "He could come back any time!"

They scrambled blindly through the tree looking for
the tunnel. As high as they were, the branches were much
thinner. The sun broke through the foliage in bright bursts,
blinding them as they moved back and forth from shadow
into light. They didn't get very far, though, before they knew
something was wrong.

"Hey, I can't move!" Ghoulie yelped.

"Me neither!" Scilla squealed as she tried to pull her
arms free.

"We're caught in a web," Beamer yelled, "—a big one!"

"Molgotha's got another web?" Scilla cried.

"Either that or she's twins," Ghoulie groaned, remembering how Mrs. Drummond had turned out to be triplets.

They shouted for help until their voices turned to
sandpaper. Nobody heard them.

*   *   *   *   *

One hour passed, then two. Beamer flinched every time
a branch rocked or a gust of wind churned up the leaves.
He was sure that Molgotha was coming for a few slurps of
human juice.

Of course, you can be scared out of your wits for only
so long. "Looks like we're going to be grounded again,"
Beamer croaked with a crooked grin and a shrug. The sun
was already dipping below the treetops.

"I wonder what we were going to have for dinner," said
Ghoulie.

"Considering our present predicament, that's not a good
subject," grumbled Beamer.

"I don't suppose we can hope that Molgotha is nice like

Charlotte, the spider from *Charlotte's Web?*" Scilla asked dejectedly. "I was just beginning to look forward to my first better-than-average report card."

"What are you worried about, Bruzelski?" asked Ghoulie. "There aren't enough juices in you for one good slurp. Molgotha will probably just step right over you."

"So I'll just shrivel up from dehydration?" she shot back at him. "Thanks for the encouragement."

"It's really not all that uncomfortable," Beamer said as he wiggled to make the web bounce. "Sort of like sitting in a hammock."

"Oh, good grief!" Ghoulie said with a huge sigh.

"Might as well catch up on my reading while I wait for dinner," Beamer said as he raised Dr. Franck's book. Beamer was glued to the giant spiderweb from his elbows back, but his forearms and hands were free. It wasn't easy, but he managed to flip the pages to where the wrinkling started. He scrunched up his face thoughtfully: "Four years and two months ago, huh? Now that I think about it, that's about the time his wife died."

Scilla jerked her head around and screwed up her face thoughtfully. "D'ya suppose those wrinkled pages and all those ink smears were caused by ... tears?"

"That's what I think," said Beamer as he struggled to turn a few more pages. "A few months later, the wrinkling gets less. Hey! Here's when he starts a new project. It's called, 'Time Machine.'"

"Whoa! That's pretty spooky," Scilla said. "Isn't that what he called Alana's aging?"

No one said anything for several minutes. Then—"How

long do you suppose before he finally decides to do whatever he's gonna do?" Scilla asked weakly, looking through the branches toward the dark attic window.

"Could be any time," Beamer said. "He can't just leave her there sleeping forever."

"Not that whatever he does is going to get us out of this predicament," grumbled Ghoulie. "What's that?!" he cried out suddenly.

Beamer heard the panic in Ghoulie's voice. The web bounced a little and then a dark shadow crossed above them.

They all screeched and screamed at once!

Some heavy-duty praying—at least a few moments of silence—might be appropriate for the demise of the Star-Fighters. And, of course, if they're gone, that's "all she wrote" for Alana. It might even make a good news story if anyone ever found their shriveled remains. Not too many people climb to the top of such tall trees these days. Their only chance of discovery might be a very low-flying plane or a kite caught in the tree—one expensive enough that someone would climb way up to retrieve it.

Beamer didn't see Molgotha's disgusting body looming above them. His eyes were closed as tightly as if he'd used superglue and a coat of cement. He wasn't doing much breathing either. Given a spider's usual diet of flies and small bugs, the kids must have looked pretty tasty to the old spider.

Beamer felt the heat of the beast. A leg brushed him. Panic was building inside him like a time bomb. The web shook and jolted, but then the shaking and rustling began to fade. He should have been a cocoon by now, but he didn't feel like it. He peeped one eye open and looked around. "Hey, guys, where'd she go?"

"Shut up," said Scilla with a voice that sounded more like a squeak. "You'll draw her attention to us."

"No, I mean it," said Beamer as he opened both eyes. "She's gone!" That's when he almost fell. "Aii!" he yelped as the strands of web beneath him broke off. He grabbed a branch and held on. Then he smiled. "She cut us free!"

"What?" asked Ghoulie, who suddenly flipped over. "Yiii!" he screeched as he dangled upside down with only one strand of spider silk holding his foot.

"Why would she do that?" Scilla asked in disbelief. She squiggled around, trying to get free. "Oh ... I hate to admit it," said Scilla from the side of her mouth, "but I think you're right. She didn't notice me. I'm here just as stiff as before, so would you guys get over here and get me loose!"

That's what they eventually did. It took longer than it might have. For one thing, spider silk is stronger than steel for its size, and Molgotha's silk was pretty thick. You couldn't just snip it loose even if you happened to have some scissors. They had to wiggle each strand free from a tree branch. Another reason was that Ghoulie kept talking about how it was impossible for a spider to have set them free. "Anything that gets caught in the web—anything—the spider cocoons to be eaten later. Even another spider gets eaten if it wanders into her web. It must have been an accident."

"Ghoulie, pipe down!" Beamer said.

"In fact, she should have been here, waiting in the center of the web when we dropped in for her dinner," Ghoulie kept on saying, as if he hadn't heard Beamer. "Come to think of it, garden spiders aren't supposed to put their webs this high up in a tree either."

Finally, when Beamer and Ghoulie freed Scilla, she too almost fell down. "Men!" she grumbled. "Y'all have got no attention to detail at all. Come on, let's go get help."

As if she'd given a verbal command, a light flashed on in the attic window.

"We don't have time to go for help," Beamer sputtered. "We're gonna have to save her ourselves."

* * * * *

The good news was that Dr. Franck hadn't bothered to close the window. The bad news was that he was standing in a pool of light next to Alana, filling a syringe with a milky fluid.

Normally, kids are not known for being particularly quiet, but today was an exception. They slipped into the attic and scooted around the wall like mice, keeping in the shadows.

When the man finished filling his syringe, Scilla broke the silence. "What are you doing to Alana? She's no lab rat, ya' know!"

He looked confused, unable to see them in the dark outreaches of the attic. "I'm not trying to hurt her. I'm trying to save her!" He looked like he was speaking to a ghost, defending his actions.

"Why don't you take her to a hospital?" Scilla said, keeping up the attack. "You're no doctor—at least not that kind of doctor."

"I've tried all kinds of doctors. No one knows how to save her!" There were tears in his eyes. The man suddenly collapsed, sinking to the floor against a tall cabinet. There, with his elbows balanced on his knees, he held his head in his hands and cried. "I'm the one who caused her to be like this," he finally said between sobs. "I killed my wife and disfigured my daughter."

18

Lab Rats

It would have been easier to take if he'd said, "The sky is falling!"

Scilla was clearly rattled. "But ... but ... d'ya mean you murdered your wife?" she gasped.

"Not intentionally. She ... my wife ... brought Alana to work with her one day," he said as he struggled back to his feet. "She was only seven at the time." He walked over and leaned against the table with the computer monitors on the shelf above. "She wasn't supposed to be there. It was a maximum-security area, but my wife wanted her to see where we worked." He turned back toward the kids, still unable to see them in the shadows. It was almost as if he were talking to himself, remembering. "I was so happy to see her. I picked her up." His voice choked. "She always ... giggled when I spun her around above my head. So ... that's what I did."

"That doesn't sound like something a murderer would do," Scilla whispered to Beamer standing next to her.

"Oh, how she laughed," the man said with tears in his eyes. "But then her feet struck a bottle." His voice again broke. "The bottle flew off the shelf and broke on the floor next to my wife. I brought Alana down into my arms but froze, not knowing what to do. Soon, the alarm screamed. My wife collapsed to the floor. I set Alana down, pushing her behind me, and rushed toward my wife. But before I got to her, hands were grabbing me and pulling me away from her. I kept crying out my wife's name, trying to break free, but they pulled me back through the air lock. One glass door slammed in place before me then another, cutting me and my fellow workers off from the infected area—the area where my wife lay on the floor!"

"But what happened to Alana?" Scilla asked anxiously.

He almost lost it, his body heaving with sobs, but he fought them back and went on. "I looked through the crowd of scientists and lab technicians trying to find Alana, and then I turned back and saw her still in the room with her mother. She was so little, shorter than the lab table, that nobody had seen her disappear around to the other side of it. I screamed for someone to open the door. Then some people in those anti-contamination suits showed up and went through the air lock to get them."

Oh, yeah, Beamer thought, *now that part sounded pretty cool. I wonder what it's like, wearing one of those things that look like rumpled, plastic space suits.*

Mr. Franck took some deep breaths before he went on, talking as he walked to Alana's bedside. "It was too late for my wife. She was already ... dead. Alana, suffering less exposure to the toxic chemical, lived. In fact, she seemed fine at first.

I was so relieved. But a couple months later her skin began looking thin and pale. The chemical had caused specific cells to mutate. A month after that the first wrinkles began to appear. My daughter was racing toward old age."

"Whoa, that's awful," Beamer murmured with a gulp.

"But it doesn't sound like it was really your fault," Scilla said more loudly. "I mean, it was Alana's foot that—"

"But it wouldn't have happened if I hadn't been so stupid!" he said as he rushed back to the table and banged his fist on it. "I knew that the area was dangerous. I was careless."

The scientist's expression changed, like he suddenly realized that real people, not ghosts, were talking to him. "Who are you? What are you doing here?" he asked angrily as he walked toward them. "Are you the children who traumatized her?" he said through clenched teeth. Suddenly he grabbed Scilla and shoved her into an animal specimen cage. "I can't have you causing her any more harm." He tripped Beamer as he and Ghoulie tried to get past him. He caught Ghoulie by the back of his collar and flung him into another cage.

"We didn't come here to hurt her," Beamer protested as the man dragged him into a third cage and locked the door. "We came to help her!"

"I don't believe you," he growled at them. "I know how you children treat anyone who is ... *different*. At any rate, I can't let you stop me from doing what I have to do, even if it means that I have to break all the laws of man and God."

Whoa, that was a lot of lawbreaking. Beamer remembered the Ten Commandments, of course. But just from the few laws he heard about in Solomon Parker's case, the laws of men must be up there in the zillions.

The man's face softened, though, when he returned to his daughter. "Even as you are, you are beautiful to me, but I want you to be a normal girl—to have friends," he said gently to her.

"I am a geneticist, you know," Dr. Franck said, looking back at the kids in the cages. "I know how to do things with … the genetic code. I had only worked with plants, though, but I found a source for human DNA and began working with those genes identified with aging. It isn't legal. I could end up in jail, but I don't care as long as I can cure my daughter."

"Do you know about DNA?" Ghoulie whispered to Scilla like a talking encyclopedia.

"Yes, I know about genes and all that stuff," Scilla whispered angrily. "You may be a grade ahead of me and a genius, but I'm not stupid!"

"Okay, okay," Ghoulie whispered. "I just wasn't sure you knew that it's the DNA code that gives you stuff like the color of your eyes and hair, the shape of your face, and—"

"I got it!" whispered Scilla again.

"I've tried every variation of gene therapy I could think of trying to slow her growth rate," Alana's father said. He swallowed hard. "But nothing has worked."

Beamer didn't notice when Scilla's fingers, which were playing aimlessly on the cage door, accidentally tripped open the latch.

"I have one more drug combination to try," Alana's father said gently to his daughter, his voice breaking, "but … it is the most dangerous one of all. It might … cost you your … life." He noticeably sagged, his hands on the bed, bracing himself as he leaned over her. Then he straightened, his face taking on a harder expression, and walked back to the table. "But maybe that's just as well—better death than to live a life alone and friendless."

"But she's not friendless!" Scilla yelled at him. "We're her friends."

"Liar!" he shouted back at her. "Be quiet."

"Hey, y'all," Scilla whispered at Beamer and Ghoulie when Dr. Franck looked away. "Hey, y'all," she whispered louder.

"What?" Beamer whispered. Then he saw Ghoulie's eyes pop open. A lightbulb had definitely gone on in Ghoulie's supercharged brain.

The man again picked up the syringe.

"Don't do it, Dr. Franck," Ghoulie yelled. "You have your miracle! Go ahead. Check the latest cell activity."

"I have given her no new medications for the past two months," he answered as he wiped tears from his eyes. "There is no reason to expect that anything has changed." But he hesitated, giving Ghoulie a long look. Then he seemed to dismiss whatever he was thinking. "What do you care, anyway?"

"Listen to me, you two!" Scilla whispered again. "Animals may not be able to open these cages, but humans can."

Beamer looked at her and finally got it. "You've gotta trust in God, Mr. Franck," Beamer said as he fingered his cage latch. "I don't know how, but he will work things out for Alana. That's what my mom and dad have taught me since I was old enough to talk."

Scilla quietly slipped outside her cage to help the others.

Again, Alana's father hesitated. "Why should I believe you? You hurt my little girl."

"But we didn't mean to!" Beamer exclaimed. "We've played with Alana. We care about her. God cares about her too. I mean, I think he's the one who brought us to her. Don't do this to her!"

"No, I have to fix her," Dr. Franck said, his voice choking. Once again he looked at the level of the liquid in the syringe.

"Check the readings on the monitor!" Ghoulie shouted to him again. "I'm telling the truth!"

Suddenly Beamer got his cage door open. He ran toward the doctor. "You can't do it!" he shouted, taking him to the floor before he could inject the fluid into Alana.

While Beamer tried to wrestle the syringe out of the scientist's hand, Ghoulie burst out of his cage and ran over to the monitor. He hit a key to display Alana's current cell activity. "Look, Dr. Franck! Here it is, just like I said."

Dr. Franck, who had just grabbed back his syringe, looked up at the screen and gasped. "I don't understand it." He let go of Beamer, stood up, and walked over to the screen. He tapped some more keys, looked at a screen showing Alana's cells two months ago, and tapped the keyboard again to see the current results. "You're right. The cells are not mutating as quickly as they were the last time I tested her. In fact, they look almost normal!"

Beamer looked knowingly at his buddies. *It might not fit into the scientist's manual of cause and effect, but some things are beyond science. Yep, science was a wonderful thing. After all, God had given humans all of creation for making things to improve our lives. But this time, the tree and the tree ship had worked with a science beyond the five senses.*

Dr. Franck was crying again, but these were happy tears as he hugged his still-sleeping daughter.

19

Beginnings and Endings

Like all holidays, this one had to end. And, as
was usual for kids, it ended with the start of school.
As they were about to walk by Alana's Pink Palace,
Beamer wondered what would happen to her. *Alana
may no longer be aging at the speed of light, but she still
looked like the Wicked Witch of the West.*

"Do you suppose Alana will ever be able to leave
this house?" Scilla said as they passed the gate.

"They can do some pretty amazing things with
plastic surgery these days," Ghoulie said, "once her
aging stabilizes and her face stops morphing."

"Maybe so," Beamer said with a worried look.
Being "different" at all can be a hard road for any kid.

The Star-Fighters were all "different." Beamer
used to think that was a bad thing until last summer.
Thanks to Old Lady Parker, the tree, and the tree
ship, they'd learned that being different was often a

good thing. You see, God created each person with their own special set of gifts.

Alana was definitely different, but Beamer didn't think that being ugly was one of her gifts. Maybe she had some gifts that would make up for her being ugly. A lot of cures for disease and inventions had been discovered by people who had diseases or problems themselves.

They were surprised to see that Alana's walk-in gate was wide open. Ms. Warrington stood about halfway up the walk, waving for them to come in. Puzzled by her strange expression, they followed her around the walkway and through the row of Italian cypress trees.

Alana was standing in the center of a large flower garden shaped like a wagon wheel, her back to them. Alana's nanny smiled at them and said, "I was hoping you'd let Alana walk to school with you. Maybe you could introduce her to some of the children. She doesn't know anyone, of course."

That was when Alana turned to face them. They all flinched and sucked in their breath. She looked even worse than before. Her nose was longer and more twisted, and her chin jutted out about as far as her nose.

Beamer had expected anything but this. *Oh, man, this isn't gonna be easy.* He watched as the poor girl reached up to cradle her face in her hands. But instead of crying, he heard laughter. Then she took off her face! Beamer blinked and opened his eyes wide. What he saw now was not a pretty face but at least a pleasant face. She still had wrinkles, although they were clearly fading.

Alana and Ms. Warrington were all laughing like their sides were going to split. *Very funny.*

Suddenly Beamer, Scilla, and Ghoulie broke into laughter too, and they all split their sides together.

"Well," whispered Scilla as she leaned over to speak in Beamer's ear, "at least we already know 'pretty' goes a lot deeper in her than it does in most girls."

Yeah, that was true. Part of Beamer even missed the old Alana. He didn't want to get all mushy or anything, but some of her wrinkled expressions had a way about them. Beauty was definitely a gift, but most people who had it seemed to think they deserved some kind of award for having it. What did they think a *gift* was all about?

Beamer saw Scilla brace herself as Alana ran up to give her a big hug. This was going to be interesting. Scilla was strictly on the outs with girls who wore frilly dresses. Maybe it would be all right if Scilla could talk her into wearing something besides pink once in a while.

Ms. Warrington signaled Beamer and Ghoulie. They followed her a few feet away from where Alana and Scilla were laughing and giggling. "You know, I have a lot to thank you kids for," she said, putting her hands on their shoulders. "As you can see, Alana's rapid aging has stopped and its effects seem to be fading. It's a miracle!" Then her expression became more serious and she lowered her voice almost to a whisper. "Her father, however, has been arrested for practicing medicine without a license. Actually, he turned himself in.

"Alana is pretty sad about it," the woman said. "He'll probably have to spend some time in jail, but he's already changed quite a bit and I think he'll come back a better man and a better father. In the meantime, I'll be taking care of Alana. I've always thought of her as my child anyway."

Alana practically danced along the sidewalk. She was so happy to be going to school with the other kids. *Man, did she have a lot to learn. Nobody over ten ever liked going to school, especially after having been on vacation.*

Beamer looked up into the trees when they reached the corner of Parkview Court. Somewhere back along the passage in those trees was the house with the disappearing forest of animals, fairies, and at least one bug-ugly gargoyle. Someday soon the Star-Fighters were going to have to search for that house. After all, you don't run into weird places like that every day ... except maybe on Murphy Street.

*   *   *   *   *

The ancient creature saw them a few minutes later, laughing as they walked along the path through the heart of the forest. They were pretty far away, and she could only glimpse them through the jigsaw puzzle of tree branches. She wished she could get closer to them, but she didn't dare. They'd be terrified. She hated that they had to be frightened of her. But that is the way it had always been between humans and spiders. Of course, most of her cousins didn't care. They didn't even think about it. They couldn't. They were programmed to eat and sleep and mate and survive until they had children and died.

Things were different for her. She could think. It happened long ago—on a night when fire had come from the sky. Since then she had watched her cousins live and die—whole lifetimes flashing by in just two seasons—while she lived on and on.

She trembled in her web as she remembered those first seasons. Nothing happened like it was supposed to. She'd made a web and gathered food, but when it came time to mate, she couldn't. Although her kind were among the larger in their species—sometimes as big as the palm of a human hand, she had grown to be three times as big as any would-be mate. So she didn't have children ... and she didn't die.

But there were other ways to die. She didn't think she'd make it through that first winter. She had to leave her web and the tree when the first frost came. Luckily she found a place beneath the earth—a small depression in a cave wall where she just fit. She worried about food, but found that she was big enough to eat small rats, mice, and bats. Yech! Talk about ugly!

Years passed and she grew larger. She moved her web to the top of the tree when a boy and his father built the structure in the tree. Later she discovered that when human children played in the structure, the web would glow. The good thing was that the glow attracted more creatures to her web. The bad thing was that she couldn't stay on the web while it was glowing. When the human dwelling was built beneath the tree, she moved into it, instead of the caves, during the winter. The web she built there glowed too.

No one came into that attic for several years. When someone finally did, the place erupted in pandemonium. People rushed in and out screaming. Luckily they left the attic long enough for her to slip back outside. She thought they would destroy the web in the attic, but it turned out they couldn't. She didn't know why. After that, an elderly scientist moved in and set up a laboratory next to the web. He lived there a few years, performing some experiments on the web. She didn't know what he did to it, but he died years later and the attic stayed vacant for many more years after that.

In the meantime, all her experiences taught her that she had to stay away from humans. That wasn't easy since she was so big. She thought about the caves. Spiders did live there, of course, but she wasn't that kind of spider. She was a tree spider, and that's where she planned to stay—way high up where humans never came. At least that is what she had thought, not realizing how adventurous human children could be.

Food was another problem. She was now, in fact, too big for one web to supply her needs, especially since she could no longer expect to find the rodents that had been her diet in the caves. So she built more webs in other trees. Eventually, she had a whole network of webs that would catch not only flies and insects like most webs, but birds and squirrels and other tree-climbing animals. As she moved from one web to another, she gradually carved those little tunnels through the tree branches. Strangely enough, the webs she built away from that first tree never glowed.

What is it those human children called her? Ah, yes—Molgotha. She'd heard them say it when they were trapped in the web. She didn't like the name. It was scary—not at all fitting for someone as beautiful as she. Her body was a gorgeous bright yellow, and she had dazzling yellow bands on her stockings. If the children could only see her as she really was, they wouldn't think of her as being a monstrous beast.

This web, deep in the forest, was her home now. She'd built it in an old sycamore tree. Its huge gnarly trunk was set amid a grove of wildflowers in one of the few places sunlight ever broke through the dense forest canopy. This was, in fact, the largest tree in the park, though nobody knew it. People never came this deep into the dark forest.

This time of morning, sunlight sliced through the forest shadows at a high angle, stirring up birds and butterflies to flutter around the tree and amid the flowers. It was her favorite time of day, for the shafts of light were so bright that she felt as if she were living in the middle of a great sunburst! Sometimes those beams of light looked strong enough for her to walk up them all the way to heaven. Yeah, she knew about heaven. She didn't know how. She just did.

Scilla

Beamer

Ghoulie

Character Bios

Priscilla Bruzelski:
Age: 12 / 6th grade, Hair/Eyes: dishwater-blonde/green, Height: 4'9"

"*Scilla*" refuses to be called by her full name because it's too prissy for this tomboy. She is smaller than your average twelve-year-old, but she makes up for her small stature with a fiercely independent, feisty personality. She lives with her grandmother whom she was sent to live with when her single mother remarried. She has a half-brother named Dashiell who lives with her mother and her mother's new husband. Her grandmother takes her to church every Sunday out of tradition. Scilla loves climbing trees, football, basketball, and anything that's not girly. She doesn't get along with the popular girls at school, but she doesn't mind. She has strong opinions and will fight for what she believes is right.

Benson McIntyre:
Age: 13 / 7th grade, Hair/Eyes: short, wavy, sandy brown hair/blue, Height: 5'

"*Beamer*," named from the famous "Beam me up Scotty" line in *Star Trek*, has an interest in all things science fiction. He hates his given name, so don't call him Benson. You might get a response in wry, sarcastic humor from this energetic teenager. He recently moved with his family from Southern California to Middle America. He has a younger brother named Michael and an older sister named Erin. His father, referred to as "Mr. Mac," is a theater director, and his mother is a pediatrician called "Dr. Mac." He loves playing on the computer, likes keeping up with the times, and considers himself on the cutting edge. Coming from a strong Christian family, he analyzes all problems with deep spiritual thought. His love for science extends to his speech, as he often speaks in sci-fi space metaphors.

Garfunkel Ives:
Age: 12 / 7th grade, Hair/Eyes: black/brown, Height: 4'10"

"*Ghoulie*" got his name from the wide-eyed look he makes when he is excited. He's an intelligent boy who skipped a grade. He's small for his age and is the typical nerd who loves gadgets and computers, which makes him fodder for bullies. The constant bullying makes him jaded and sarcastic, and he would love to get revenge on the bullies. His father is a successful CFO of a large corporation and his mother is a highly-respected lawyer. His parents have little time for a spiritual life — or him — and have left his upbringing to the nanny. His parents have also left him with an extensive computer and gadget collection which he loves to use to quench his thirst for scientific knowledge.

There's a Spaceship in My Tree!

Robert West

1

Alien

Beamer was an alien. He wasn't a ten-legged slime bag with fourteen eyes, unless, of course, you believed his big sister. Still, Beamer was an alien—no question about it. He didn't belong here. He couldn't even breathe here.

His mom said it was just the humidity. Sure! Methane was more like it! When they found his shriveled, oxygen-deprived body, they'd be sorry.

Now he'd been sent to some place called a cellar—clearly an alien environment. Nobody in California had a cellar.

Beyond the small pool of murky light at the foot of the steps, a heavy gloom spread out across the room like a fog bank. He stepped down from the last creaking step. "Hey!" he yelped, recoiling back up the step. "What *is* this stuff?"

He kneeled down to test the floor with his fingers. *Weird, man ... spongy, like maybe it wasn't a floor at all but something alive, like a tongue for something with a digestive system!*

Dust was what it really was—several years' buildup. Beamer stepped down again hesitantly, sending a puff of it into the air. The wind outside picked up, rattling the high, grime-coated windows. The structure above him creaked and groaned like a cranky old woman.

Then something scritched and scratched. He turned ... and froze!

It was huge, with tentacles attached to a disgustingly bloated body. Not a second too soon, Beamer dived to the floor to avoid a twisted tentacle reaching over his head.

Now, point-blank in front of him, was a large bin of shiny, black rocks—no doubt the shrunken, dehydrated remains of creatures the beast had already devoured.

Beamer scooted back frantically on all fours. At the same moment, a high whining sound came from behind. He lurched to his feet and whirled around, bumping into a cart, which sped rapidly away. Suddenly he was pelted in the face by a strangely filmy object. A moment later he was wrestling with an entire barrage of filmy, flimsy, smelly things.

Aiiii! *Germ warfare*! his mind screamed.

There was a screech. "*Yiiiii*!" Beamer yelped, as a small creature flashed by. It leapt to a table and fled through a break in a window.

Beamer shot up the steps like a missile and blew through a door into a short hallway. He slammed the door behind him and leaned against the opposite wall, breathing heavily.

"Mother!" A shrill voice from upstairs brought him spinning around in panic. "Did you know they've got a vacuum laundry chute up here?" The voice continued. "Shoots clothes down to the basement like spit wads!"

Beamer's mother stood in the entryway wearing tattered, cut-off overalls and a tool belt. "Well, at least something works around here. Beamer!" she exclaimed in amazement, "What are you wearing on your ear?"

"Huh?" Beamer removed a pair of girl's underwear from his left ear—*Vacuum laundry chute? Whoever heard of a vacuum laundry chute?*—and threw them down disgustedly.

"Hey, Mom!" the shrill voice called again. "I can't find my pink Nikes." It was Beamer's big sister, Erin. At fourteen going on fifteen, she was God's self-proclaimed gift to the ninth grade. Of course, that was back in Katunga Beach. Middleton was a whole new ball game.

That's what this alien world was called—Middleton—a middle-sized city in a middle-sized state, smack dab in the middle of Middle America—a thousand miles from the nearest beach!

Only a week ago, Beamer was hanging out in a cool, high-rolling suburb of L.A. on the cutting edge of the early teen set. Now he was carting boxes around a broken-down house in a prehistoric neighborhood on an ancient street probably named for somebody's dog. Murphy Street. It certainly wasn't Shadow Beach Lane.

Beamer scrunched up his nose. The house even smelled old—as in fossilized. The discovery of an electrical outlet had been a great relief. He wasn't sure Xbox came in a windup version.

He banged through the screen door onto the front porch and picked up another carton. His mother was standing there, holding a scraggly plant in a pig-shaped pot.

The lady realtor who had given it to her was bustling toward her car, her mouth on auto-speak. "If you run into anything unusual," she called, "don't panic. I'm sure it's not dangerous. The previous residents were … uh … different—scientists or rock singers or something—but harmless. Anyway, just call if you have a question."

"I will," Beamer's mother responded absently, still looking in bewilderment at the ugly pot.

Beamer looked at the ramshackle porch swing and the peeling paint around the windows. *Rock singers in this dive? Who did she think she was kidding?* Then again, that same lady had managed to sell this overgrown pile of bricks to his otherwise genetically superior parents.

Beamer MacIntyre shifted the box in his arms, pried open the screen door with his pinkie, and spun through into the house. The antique door immediately fell off its hinges. Mrs. MacIntyre, or Dr. Mac, as her kiddie patients called her, groaned and pulled a screwdriver from her tool belt.

Beamer trudged slowly up the staircase with his load. "Move, you dunderhead," his sister growled as she pounded down past him like an avalanche. "Mother, isn't this place air-conditioned? I'm about to die!"

"It's the humidity, honey," her mother answered. "You'll get used to it."

"Mo-o-o-o-ommm!" Erin wailed, charging into the crate-littered living room. "D'you mean there's no air-conditioning?!"

"No, I mean you'll get used to the humidity," Dr. Mac replied. "Air-conditioning is being installed—one for upstairs and one for downstairs. Your father is out arranging things now. Last I heard the downstairs one will be working tomorrow."

"What about the upstairs one?" Erin asked with a shrill note of panic.

"Uhm . . . not for a couple of weeks, I'm afraid."

"Weeks!!! So I'm supposed to wake up every morning with my hair dripping? That does it; I can't start school—not 'til the air conditioner's working."

"Calm down, honey," her mother said. "Your hair always

looks just fine. I'm more concerned about whether that oversized octopus of a coal-burning, water-heating furnace in the basement will keep us warm in winter."

Octopus? Furnace?! Beamer cast a glance down at the basement door, his cheeks picking up a definite reddish glow. *Oh great! So I had a battle with a furnace! What were those little black things then? At least nobody saw me ... I hope.*

"Now go finish unpacking. I'm sure your shoes will show up," Dr. Mac said, turning her daughter around and pointing her back up the steps. "Go on."

Erin groaned and lumbered up the staircase, then accelerated past Beamer to the top. She triumphantly stuck her tongue out at him and yanked open a door.

Beamer finally reached the second floor. Straight ahead was a wide but short hallway with two doors on the left and one on the right that opened into bedrooms. Immediately to the right of the staircase was a short, narrow hallway that led to the upstairs bathroom and a spare bedroom beyond. He kicked open the door to his room—the second one on the left—and promptly tripped over something in the doorway. "Oomph!" he gasped as he and the box's contents simultaneously thudded to the floor.

Groaning, he propped himself up to see the spilled items strewn, like a comet's tail, across the floor toward the tall, twin front windows. Through a window he noticed clouds gathering above the rooftops. *Back in L.A. we had rain programmed down to just one season a year. Here I am, two time zones and half a continent away from home.* "Marooned in Middle America," he moaned out loud. "I'd rather be on Mars."

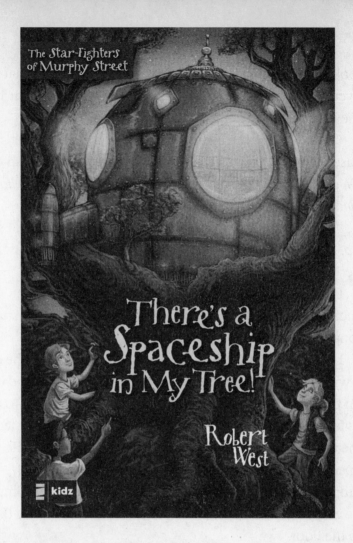

There's a Spaceship in My Tree!: Episode I
Softcover • ISBN 0310714257

Beamer, age 13, who speaks only Californian, is an alien in the world of Middle America, exiled to a bizarre, ancient house on a mysterious street that may or may not exist on any map. With the help of a nerdy African-American kid named Ghoulie, a gangly tomboy named Scilla, and a miraculous, broken-down tree house shaped like a spaceship, he battles the indigenous life forms in his new home, from bullying creatures to the strange inhabitants of dark castles, subterranean caverns, and a spider web the size of a house, to discover how God gives a distinctive purpose to each uniquely designed human being.

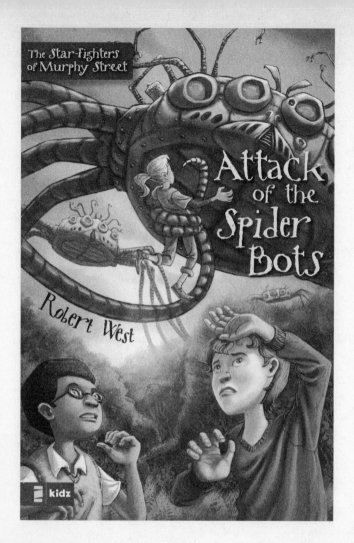

Attack of the Spider-Bots: Episode II
Softcover • ISBN 0310714265

Star-Fighters Beamer, Ghoulie, and Scilla follow a strange clanking sound in their cave labyrinth and stumble onto a screaming one-eyed monster that chases them into a huge cavern enclosing a fully animated miniature world. Their search for the person who created that world leads them on a wild adventure to a palatial mansion within a wintry jungle that hides a terrible secret—a secret that they will have to trust God to expose.

We want to hear from you. Please send your comments about this book to us in care of zreview@zondervan.com. Thank you.

ZONDERVAN.com/
AUTHORTRACKER
follow your favorite authors